She was so wounded, and so fiercely defensive about keeping people away from her, yet the woman standing there at the door, ready to bolt, didn't fool him at all.

Not for a minute. She wanted what he wanted to give her—and, unless he was totally mistaken, she loved him.

He turned back and finally did what he'd wanted to do all along. He pulled Bella into his arms and kissed her—not in a friendly little gesture, as he'd done before, but in the way a man needed to kiss a woman. Crushing her hard to his body, he lowered his head to her and sought her lips with a hunger that surprised him. Prying open her mouth with his tongue, he sought the deep recesses, felt her respond with her own tongue, heard just the slightest whimper of a moan escape her as she wound her fingers around his neck and held him there. Pressed her hips to his in a carnal way that caused him to go erect immediately and groan aloud, with no thought whatsoever about where they were and who might be watching them…

Now that her children have left home, **Dianne Drake** is finally finding the time to do some of the things she adores—gardening, cooking, reading, shopping for antiques. Her absolute passion in life, however, is adopting abandoned and abused animals. Right now Dianne and her husband Joel have a little menagerie of three dogs and two cats, but that's always subject to change. A former symphony orchestra member, Dianne now attends the symphony as a spectator several times a month and, when time permits, takes in an occasional football, basketball or hockey game.

Recent titles by the same author:

THE WIFE HE'S BEEN WAITING FOR
A BOSS BEYOND COMPARE
ITALIAN DOCTOR, FULL-TIME FATHER
A FAMILY FOR THE CHILDREN'S DOCTOR
THEIR VERY SPECIAL CHILD

DR VELASCOS' UNEXPECTED BABY

BY
DIANNE DRAKE

MILLS & BOON

First published in Great Britain 2009
Large Print edition 2009
Harlequin Mills & Boon Limited,
Eton House, 18-24 Paradise Road,
Richmond, Surrey TW9 1SR

© Dianne Despain 2009

ISBN: 978 0 263 20553 4

Set in Times Roman 16½ on 18½ pt.
17-1209-56942

Harlequin Mills & Boon policy is to use papers that are
natural, renewable and recyclable products and made
from wood grown in sustainable forests. The logging and
manufacturing process conform to the legal environmental
regulations of the country of origin.

Printed and bound in Great Britain
by CPI Antony Rowe, Chippenham, Wiltshire

DR VELASCOS'
UNEXPECTED
BABY

CHAPTER ONE

"Everything checks out fine, Dr. Burke." Dr. Raul Navarro gave Bella an encouraging smile as he handed her a prescription for eardrops. "It's just a reaction to flying, a little congestion in the eustachian tube. It happens all the time, and it's nothing to worry about. But it's better to treat it now than let it go."

Fly to Peru, get an earache. Of all the rotten luck. "I'm not worried about it so much as frustrated. My timing's lousy, isn't it? I haven't been sick one day in five years, not even with a simple cold, and yet here I am…" She gestured to the tiny office. "The first thing I have to do when I get off the plane is go see a doctor."

Navarro chuckled. "It's true what they say, you know. Doctors *do* make the worst patients. But I promise you, in another day or two, with the eardrops, you'll be as good as new. So, what kind of medicine did you say you practice?"

"Pediatrics. I specialize in children under the age of six."

"It takes someone special to handle the children. I thought about going into pediatrics for about a minute. Then I was assigned to work in the pediatric ward during my first rotation as an intern, and that's when I learned I had no talent for it. Children are these little balls of mystery, and if you're not a good detective who can solve that mystery pretty quickly, the child can suffer. It's easier for me to simply have my adult patient list symptoms and point me in the direction of what's ailing them."

"But children point, too. Just in different ways. It's all in what you know and what you perceive, I suppose."

"Or where your special talent comes in. With children, you've either got it, or you haven't. I don't, which is why I'm treating you and not the Menendez twins, who come in every few days for one thing or another. So, use the drops and by tomorrow you should notice an appreciable difference. That plugged-up feeling will start to disappear and the popping you're experiencing will stop. Of course, you already know that, ddin't you? Working with children, I'll bet you treat more ear infections than I do. So, what brings you here?" he asked as he made the last of his notes in the chart. "Holiday? Visiting friends?"

"Just looking around. Curiosity, mostly." And closure. "My sister loved Peru, and I thought I'd come see what she fell in love with."

"Well, your sister has very good taste. I was gone for several years when I was in medical school and I came right back." Finishing his charting, the doctor handed it to the office nurse then led Bella through the hall to the waiting room.

Rounding the corner, she bumped straight into a man with a baby in his arms. A very loud baby at that. A cry that caught her attention, except she wasn't on duty. "I'm sorry," she said, stepping back from him as he pulled the infant tighter to his chest.

More intent on the doctor, the man didn't seem to notice Bella. "Raul, where's the pediatric clinic?" he asked Dr. Navarro.

"Gabriel, my friend…" Dr. Navarro started, then glanced at the bundle in his arms. "And who do we have here?"

"Ana Maria," Gabriel said. "Two days old, and she needs a doctor."

"I didn't know you had…" Dr. Navarro said, signaling his nurse forward as Bella instinctively stepped closer to take a look at the child. But Gabriel pulled even further away from her. A very natural, protective gesture Bella recognized from so many parents of her tiny patients.

"Who's your pediatrician?" Gabriel persisted.

He seemed more flustered than frightened, Bella thought, as most parents of newborns like his usually were. She saw it all the time in her pediatric practice—when a brand-new infant sneezed or coughed, the parents went to pieces. Sometimes to the point of being irrational or inconsolable. But it was all fear. She understood that, and sympathized with the man.

"Sorry, Gabriel, but he's not in today," Dr. Navarro replied when Gabriel had told him. "I could have one of our general practitioners take a look at her, though. Or perhaps I could…"

"Or I could take a look," Bella offered without giving it a thought.

Both men looked at her. Dr. Navarro smiled, while the man he called Gabriel frowned. "That's right," Doctor Navarro said. "You *are* a pediatrician. So, you wouldn't mind doing this? Because I'd appreciate your help, especially considering what you already know about my way with babies."

Before Bella could reply, Gabriel thrust the baby into her arms. "Her name's Ana Maria. She's two days old," he said. "Closer to three now."

"I'm Dr. Arabella Burke," she responded, although she was sure he wasn't paying that much attention to her. His focus was on the office nurse, who'd thrust a chart at him with a patient history to fill out. "Call me Bella," she continued, but more to Ana Maria than to Ana Maria's father, who was scribbling furiously now.

Pulling the blanket back from the baby's face as she followed Dr. Navarro to an empty exam room, she looked into the face of an angel. A beautiful, perfect little angel. And things felt…right. Right for the first time since Rosie had died. The power of a baby, she thought. A baby who needed her. Or maybe it was the other way around.

Sniffing Ana Maria's breath, Bella turned up her nose at the unmistakable smell. Curdled milk! The baby had a tummyache from curdled milk, which gave the poor little thing every right to cry the way she was doing. "What are you feeding her?" Bella asked Gabriel, her full attention on her tiny patient, although she did chance one brief glance into the adult version of her tiny patient's eyes. Beautiful eyes, both father and daughter.

"Milk," he answered. He handed the paperwork back to the nurse then positioned himself where he was able to look directly over Bella's shoulder, moving in so close to her they were practically pressed together. So close she could smell the wonderful scent of his aftershave. Lime? She wasn't sure, but it had a nice crispness to it that suited his crisp edge. And it was nothing to admire in a married man with a sick baby!

"As in…what kind of milk? Mother's milk?" She seriously doubted that was the case, judging from what she smelled on Ana Maria. "Cow's milk?" Laying a gentle hand across the baby's chest, she turned to look at Gabriel, this time giving him a full appraisal. Handsome man. Large. Broad shoulders. She liked the look of the locals…liked it very much, especially on *this* local. Ana Maria took after her father in her looks, and Bella couldn't help but think that Gabriel's wife must be beautiful, too. "Soy milk, maybe?"

He cleared his throat nervously. "Goat's milk. Raw."

"Raw goat's milk?" That did surprise her. But there were cultural differences in Peru from those she was used to. She understood that, especially in the more rural areas. That was one of the diversities her sister had loved here. Yet Bella didn't really peg Gabriel for the rural type. Not in the way he dressed, not in his precisely tailored haircut or the finely buffed finish of his fingernails. Not in the expensive leather dress shoes he wore or the silver wristwatch on his left wrist, which probably cost more than many people here made in an entire year. "Well, she isn't tolerating the goat's milk," Bella said. "It might be an allergy to it, or it simply could be that the milk is too harsh for her newborn system. My suggestion would be to have her mother switch to breastfeeding, if that's possible, and if it's not…"

"Her mother died in childbirth. My mother has a goat, and that's the only available milk."

Blunt words, and startling. And his face was so dispassionate, the tone of his voice so thorny when he spoke that Bella shivered from his tragedy, from her own… "I'm…I'm so sorry. I didn't know." That explained the goat's milk, though.

"Why should you?" he snapped. "You don't know me, I don't know you. How the hell would you know anything?"

Surprise, mixed with sympathy and indignation, assailed her over his reaction. People grieved, people got angry over the death of a loved one, and she'd dealt with all the emotions herself these past weeks. That's why she was here in Peru now—to deal with the emotions. But she was seeing something else in Gabriel, something she couldn't even guess at. She blinked hard, trying to disconnect herself from the growing opinion that this man was just plain ill mannered. He'd lost his wife, for heaven's sake, and he was grieving. He also had a sick little girl to deal with, so if ever there was a reason to be rude, this man had it, and her heart did go out to him. "No, I don't know you. But I'm still very sorry for your loss."

"I…um…" A deep sigh followed by a barely perceptible wince escaped him as he glanced down at Ana Maria, who'd finally quit crying for the moment. "I didn't mean to be so…" He ran an impatient hand through his hair. "Do you have any formula suggestions, Doctor? I don't know enough about what's available to make a good choice. And I'm sorry for—"

"No need for an apology. I understand." She'd lost her sister and three friends only two months ago, and in the past few weeks she'd snapped at people the way he did, taken offense where none had been intended, and had found herself apologizing profoundly for her irrational behavior on many occasions.

So, yes, she did understand. Her suffering was unquestionably different from his, but she did know what it felt like to hurt so very deeply and suffer long and hard from it, and her heart ached for this man, for what lay ahead of him. "No need to apologize at all," she continued. "And as far as a formula for Ana Maria goes, I don't know what's available here, but my preference for a little while would be something soy-based, just until her doctor can determine what kind of intolerance she's built up. Back in the States, there's a particular product I usually recommend, especially for newborns, and I'd like to see if we can—"

He held out his hand to stop her. "Done. I'll get the formula. Give me the name and I'll get it here. Have it overnighted."

A man of action. She liked that decisiveness in him. In some people it more resembled arrogance but in Gabriel it was…sexy. Except she wasn't going to think sexy in terms of a man who'd just lost his wife. It was wrong. Just plain wrong.

Clearing her throat, hoping the diversion would clear her mind of those uninvited thoughts, Bella snapped her head toward the window and fixed her gaze on a boy in the street. He was playing with a dog...brown and white spots. Cute boy. Cute dog. *Focus, Bella.* Just... focus. A deep breath steadied her as she looked back at Gabriel...concentrating on one of his shirt buttons, mid-chest. "Overnighted... good. Let me write down the name of a distributor I know, and you can tell him you talked to me. He's usually responsive to my referrals." She lifted her gaze to his chin then finally to his eyes again. So dark and...deep. *Focus, Bella.* "And in the meantime, to feed Ana Maria, I'd suggest—"

"Sugar water," he volunteered.

He was staring at her...his brown eyes into her green ones. Causing shivers. Goose bumps up and down her arms. *Focus, Bella.* It was merely a sympathy reaction. "Yes, sugar water is good. As long as you keep her hydrated she'll be fine with that for a little while, and I think giving her tummy time to settle down is wise at this point.

Babies usually tolerate sugar water quite well." There were different things she might have tried if they were someplace else, but they were here, and the simple approach seemed the best, given the circumstances. Besides, Gabriel was competent. He exuded that, and so much more, which put her at ease with her decision. "And you're going to be just fine," she said to Ana Maria, as she picked her up and held her close for a moment, savoring the feel of having a baby in her arms. Savoring the baby smell of her, too.

Dear God, she missed medical practice. It had been two months and it seemed like two years. She needed to get back. "Look, I don't work here, or I'd advise keeping Ana Maria under observation for a few hours, just to make sure she doesn't start vomiting or get dehydrated. Let me talk to Dr. Navarro, and maybe he'll have a suggestion."

Almost against her will, Bella placed the baby back into Gabriel's arms. "Another trained eye is always good in situations like this, so let me…"

"I'd appreciate that. But I don't want her first few days of life to be spent under watch in a medical facility. She deserves…better from me." There was no animosity in his voice. He wasn't arguing the point, merely explaining it. And his voice broke with those words, causing Bella's heart to lurch. Yet what she saw…the way he held the baby wasn't as nurturing as she would have expected. Or as protective. Ana Maria was pulled close to his body, but it was a stiff gesture, one done more from obligation, or from textbook learning, than his natural desire to take care of this child.

Honestly, that did puzzle her. Of course, she hadn't lived his life these past few days. Hadn't experienced his traumas and emotions. Perhaps he was frightened of becoming too attached to his child, especially after the death of his wife. And now that his daughter was sick…yes, his stiffness was certainly understandable, but even one as young as Ana Maria sensed that and Bella feared what might come of what Ana Maria was feeling right now…her daddy's uneasiness.

Easy, Bella. This isn't your medical practice. The man Dr. Navarro had called Gabriel was a stranger and his daughter was not her patient. Other than a quick exam as a courtesy to a nice doctor who didn't have a pediatrician available, she had no business getting involved in this matter. Yet Gabriel seemed so emotionally detached, she couldn't help but speak. "You may think Ana Maria deserves better than a short stay in a hospital, and I won't argue with you there, but she also deserves to be watched by someone who's qualified to see complications and signs and symptoms, and I believe—"

"I appreciate your concern, but I'm physician—well, surgeon, actually," he interrupted. "Not a pediatrician, but I have enough skills to look after a baby."

So he was a fellow medic? Now, that was a surprise. Or maybe it wasn't. The man she was seeing here, right this very minute, wasn't himself. He was under an extraordinary amount of stress. But, yes, she *could* imagine him as a doctor, especially when she took another look at his hands...nice hands. Gentle. Smooth. They certainly looked like the hands of a surgeon. "You're a physician under a lot of stress," she said sympathetically. "And while I'm sure, under normal circumstances, that you're very good at what you do, these aren't normal circumstances, Doctor..."

"Velascos. Gabriel Velascos."

"And I'm Arabella Burke," she told him again. This time he was definitely paying attention. "Most people call me Bella."

His smile turned warm for a fraction of a second. "That's a pity. Arabella is a lovely name. It suits you, *Arabella*."

His voice dropped its pitch just a fraction. Went smooth and silky, like a fine cognac. Was he actually flirting with her? His wife had been dead less than three days and he was already flirting?

It caught her off guard, shocked her. Under different circumstances she might have been flattered by it. But under *these* circumstances she wasn't sure what she felt, and in response she donned her best, most professional expression. "I'd still like to have someone else observe Ana Maria for a little while, since you're emotionally involved." But maybe not as much as he should have been. Unfortunately, all her initial good impressions of Dr. Gabriel Velascos were starting to melt away, and now she wasn't sure what she was feeling. Pity, for sure. And a little anger mixed in. Maybe some confusion, too. "I'll be back in a moment, Dr. Velascos, after I've consulted with Dr. Navarro."

With that, Bella escaped into the hall, all too glad to be away from the very puzzling Dr. Gabriel Velascos. All too breathless over him too, which made no sense whatsoever.

* * *

Well, he'd called it right. Thank God Ana Maria's problem was only an intolerance to the goat's milk, as he'd expected. That was easily fixed. And the rest of it…one step at a time. One lousy step at a time. He'd get her milk intolerance straightened out, then think about what came after that. That's all he could do—just take care of the baby the best way he knew how.

"A baby. I have a baby." *Dear God, what was he going to do with a baby?* Yesterday he'd been a man without attachments, today he had a baby. His sister's baby. "A baby."

Saying the words out loud, or thinking them…either way, his breath caught in his throat for an instant, threatening to asphyxiate him with the complications of what those four simple words meant—*I have a baby*. "A baby…Lynda's baby. *My* baby." He whispered the words reluctantly, trying them on the way he tried on a pair of new shoes—cautiously at first, to see if they fit, then, only after they did, deciding if they were comfortable enough to keep. The only thing was, if a pair of shoes didn't fit, he always had the option of asking for another size or simply walking away from the store empty-handed. But with this baby—*Ana Maria*—no matter how much she didn't fit his lifestyle, and there was definitely no give in there for her whatsoever, he couldn't just send her back and ask for another size, or walk away altogether. Lynda had been so excited to have a child…she'd cherished her pregnancy, lived for the moment she gave birth. So many times over the months she'd told him how being a mother was her destiny, so how could he walk away from that? How could he walk away from what had meant the world to her? And from his own flesh and blood?

He couldn't. That was his answer, and also his problem. Ana Maria's father had walked away, but he couldn't. "My baby," he said one more time, hoping that by saying the words they would somehow bring about a magical change in his dilemma…like Lynda really being alive, or Hector having a change of heart and welcoming his new baby girl into his family after all.

Neither of those things were going to happen, though. Practicality was one of the traits he counted on most when nothing else worked, and, being the practical man he considered himself to be, he couldn't see anything else working here. No miracles. No flights of fancy or fantasy. He had a baby now. And nothing changed the fact that those simple words were causing his stomach to churn, his head to pound, his whole world to spin, and his destiny to be cast into directions he'd never looked forward to for himself. Not like this, anyway.

His baby, maybe. But what the hell was he going to do about it?

"We'll get it figured out," he whispered to Ana Maria. He didn't look at her, though. Not too closely. For now it was best to keep her at a distance. Protect her, care for her, but keep the emotional attachment under check until he could figure out what to do. "Whatever happens, Ana Maria, I promise that no matter what I do, it will be in your best interests. You deserve better than what you've had so far, and I'll make sure you get it." It was a promise he took to heart, and one he didn't know how to fulfill.

Finally chancing a quick glimpse of the baby in his arms, Gabriel caught her looking up at him, her big eyes full of…was that trust? No, babies that age didn't trust. They couldn't even focus. For the most part they merely existed, and responded to their environment. The way Ana Maria was looking at him right now was only a response, probably to his voice. She wasn't used to hearing a man's voice, that's all. But when he risked another quick look to confirm his diagnosis…damn it, he was positive he saw trust again. "Don't do that," he warned. "Not with me, because it won't work, Ana Maria. You can look at me that way all you want, but it's not going to work."

Her eyes were so beautiful, though. As beautiful as Arabella's eyes which, he thought, had been the most beautiful eyes he'd ever seen. Except in Arabella's he saw sadness. She held it back, but it was there, and he did wonder what made such beautiful eyes so sad.

Pulling Ana Maria a little closer to him, he assumed a natural rocking action, waiting for Arabella to return, and within seconds Ana Maria was fast asleep in his arms. If only life really was that simple.

"They really don't have the facilities here in the clinic to keep her, but Dr. Navarro said he'd have his office nurse watch her for a couple of hours to make sure she's getting along better." It wasn't a perfect solution, but it would do. And the baby would be under observation for a short time, which made Bella feel a lot better. Gabriel was also a doctor with so much emotional turmoil, and Bella knew, better than most, how that could play on good judgment. She was glad Nurse Melaina Juarez had agreed to keep watch for a while.

"Look, I'm grateful for everything you've done, Arabella. I think that while they're looking after Ana Maria here, I'll go and make arrangements for the formula to be sent."

"So before you leave, maybe later today, would you like me to have another look at her?"

He shook his head. "You've done more than most people would have, and I'm sure you have things you'd rather be doing than looking after a stranger."

Things she dreaded doing. Things she wanted to put off doing. "Yes, I do, actually. But to be blunt, Doctor, I don't think you're reacting normally to Ana Maria right now. You're…too stiff. You know, doing what's required but not with the emotional nurturing she needs from you. She's a beautiful little girl yet you hold her like she's made of plastic…a plastic doll. And you seem to respond to her, but in a very stilted way. Which worries me. You said you'd take care of her and maybe you mean that, but I get the feeling that taking care of a newborn is the last thing you want to do. In which case I think it might become very easy for you to overlook something in her condition. And I'm not implying that you'd mean to do it, because I don't think you would intentionally. But with what you've just been through, things aren't normal for you now, and you're not responding as you normally would."

OK, so maybe she was overstepping the line here, but she was concerned because she knew how it felt to go through the motions without really thinking about them, which was what Gabriel seemed to be doing. You did what you needed to do but without any emotional invest-ment. It was like walking through a fog—your senses were distorted, you couldn't be sure in which direction you were headed. If you were alone it didn't matter so much, but Gabriel wasn't alone. And she did recognize that fog around him, which was why she felt compelled to react.

"You're very quick with accusations, aren't you? Especially when none of this concerns you!"

"Then tell me I'm wrong. That's all it will take,

Dr. Velascos, and I'll be satisfied that you don't need my concern. Or my help."

His eyes softened for a moment. "You're a good doctor, aren't you?"

"I try to be." She wasn't sure what to make of him again. The man was vacillating between someone who fascinated her and someone who, likewise, scared her. She didn't know what it was about him…his circumstances, his natural way? But she felt drawn to him. Or maybe it was to Ana Maria.

Yes, that was it. Ana Maria was desperately in need of the emotional bond only a parent could have for a child…a bond Bella wasn't seeing in Dr. Velascos. She was reacting to that. That's all it could be. "Which is why I'm worried. It comes with the territory. I worry about all my patients." And she worried about Ana Maria, who wasn't even her patient.

"I suppose we all do, don't we?"

His comment was more offhand than direct, as if his thoughts were somewhere else. Perhaps they were. "I know this is all confusing for you, Gabriel. But it will get better, I promise. It's just going to take some time to make the adjustments and for now Ana Maria will be fine. Babies, even as young as she is, are very resilient." Odd, her need to comfort him. But he seemed like he needed encouragement from somewhere. In brief moments, he looked so…lost.

Good heavens, what was she doing, getting involved like this? Gabriel and Ana Maria were in good hands with Dr. Navarro and his nurse, and that problem was solved. But hers was not, which was why it was time to pull back the emotions. Time to quit looking for ways to put off the inevitable, and getting involved with Gabriel the way she was trying to do was just another way to avoid what she had to do. She recognized that. Accepted it. "Look, if you need something, Dr. Navarro will be able to help you. He seems like a very capable doctor and I'm sure he'll put you in touch with a good pediatrician." She pulled the blanket back from Ana Maria's face, brushed a thumb over her soft, chubby cheek, then stepped back, feeling a sudden sadness she didn't understand. "Take care of yourself, Gabriel. You and Ana Maria will have a wonderful life together."

CHAPTER TWO

SHE'D eaten a little dinner, not so much because she'd wanted it but because she'd needed it. Something about holding little Ana Maria in her arms that afternoon had filled her with a longing that scared her. That, added to the dread of what she was here to do, made her meal a necessity, but not an enjoyable one. And now, hours later, she was tired of tossing and turning, and she simply couldn't sleep. There were too many unwanted thoughts galloping through her mind, keeping her awake.

This was so hard, knowing that she was about to face the worst thing she'd ever faced in her life. Until now, she'd been able to blot out her sister's death, pretend this trip to Peru was merely a holiday where she could take a stroll through the countryside, mingle with the people, eat the cuisine, see the sights. But it wasn't that at all, and the nearness of what she needed to face in order to heal herself was pounding at her.

She wanted to do this, but could she? Could she open Rosie's clinic and make her sister's dream a reality? Being someone who always took the sure, steady path, the way she did, this seemed almost crazy. Rosie had been the one who had taken the risks, who had looked at life as an exciting mountain to climb. Bella, though, had been the one who had stuck to the flat paths, who hadn't veered off.

But she was veering in a big way now, wasn't she? It was terrifying but it seemed right, fulfilling Rosie's promise this way. If that's what she decided to do.

Bella was worried about Ana Maria, too. And about Gabriel, who probably didn't need someone like her worrying about him. Yet she worried anyway, wondering why she'd latched on to the two of them almost immediately. Possibly her need for something that made some sense in her life? Something that made sense in the middle of something so confusing? Treating a sick child made so much sense to her. But Bella didn't dismiss the possibility that fixing on Gabriel and his daughter was a distraction because she knew herself, knew how she'd wanted to avoid the obvious. Once she stepped into her sister's dream, took it on as her own, her sister would be gone forever and she couldn't face that, wasn't ready to face that.

Whatever the case, there were too many reminders around her of how fragile life could be. She understood that now, more than she had any other time in her life. She was pretty sure Gabriel did, too, and he coped by being distant. She coped by…well, that was the problem. She wasn't sure how she coped because she hadn't allowed herself that yet.

Oh, she was strong enough. It had become a requirement with the way she and Rosie had grown up orphans from an early age, being tossed into so many situations where they had been tolerated but not loved the way children deserved. She'd been strong in medical school, too, and in her medical practice. It was easy, being strong, but lately she'd wondered if that strength had been a sham. Because deep down, when it had counted, she hadn't found any of that strength she'd thought would be there. "You're a fake, Arabella Burke," she said, looking at herself in the mirror as she paced by it for the twentieth time in the past few minutes. "A great big fake who didn't even know she was faking. Which makes you pretty pathetic, doesn't it?"

She didn't stay at the mirror long enough for the image in it to reply. The truth was, she didn't need conciliatory words, or more of the lie she'd been telling herself all this time. *Mirror, mirror on the wall, who's the strongest of them all? Why, it's Bella!* Bella, the queen of self-deception.

Rather than taking on a heated debate with herself, Bella pulled on her pink chenille, floor-length bath robe, stepped into her pink bedroom slippers, and headed to the hall, determined to pace up and down until she was exhausted. A nice brisk walk, in a place without the mirror image waiting to taunt her, was good, she decided as she set off, her footsteps silent on the thick, padded carpet.

Five minutes of power-walking from one end of the hall to another didn't have the desired effect, though, because Bella felt none the worse for her near-marathon pace. But as she was about to set out on her second round by tackling the stairs, the elevator doors at the other end of the hall whooshed open and a young man in neatly pressed gray slacks and a maroon jacket scuttled out, heading straight to the first room on the left. She watched with mild interest, not because it was interesting as much as any diversion was good. It did seem awfully late to have room service delivered, though. Probably some other poor soul who couldn't sleep, asking for a glass of warm milk.

Warm milk! Why hadn't she thought of that? Perhaps its soothing effect would help her. Besides, it seemed much more appealing than running up and down the hotel stairs in her pink nightwear, trying to wear herself out. "Excuse me," she said to the room attendant, trying not to be too loud about it.

He acknowledged her with a nod as the hotel door at which he stood cracked open and he handed in a covered tray. That's when she heard it…the sound of a crying baby in the room. Naturally, her attention fixed on that as the attendant backed away from the door and the man inside thanked him.

Gabriel Velascos! She recognized his voice but she wasn't fast enough to get to the door before he shut it. A couple of loud raps remedied that, and a second later he opened the door to her, immediately blinking his obvious surprise. "Do you have built-in radar?" he asked, his voice more weary than stiff. His eyebrows did raise as he took in her pink nightwear.

"Maybe I do." He was dressed in jeans, and an unbuttoned white cotton shirt that proved a startlingly sexy contrast to his dark skin. Bare feet, mussed hair, the total image of him caused Bella to step back when he opened the door all the way. She shouldn't be harboring these kinds of thoughts for him. He had been widowed only three days, for heaven's sake! A man in mourning. He probably hadn't even had time to bury his wife yet.

Hormonal reaction, she decided. Biological clock ticking hard and fast. A particularly pointless ticking for a woman who was on a road with an uncertain ending to it. Or maybe she was finally tired. "I heard Ana Maria…"

"She's been crying for the past hour, and I can't get her to sleep. I had room service bring me sugar water because I thought she might be hungry, and if that doesn't work…" He shrugged.

Bella went straight to the crib where Ana Maria was having a royal fit, and picked her up.

"Is it your tummy again?" she practically cooed, running her fingers lightly over Ana Maria's belly to check for any distention. None found. Then she felt her cheeks and forehead for a fever and, again, none discovered. "So far, so good," she said softly, raising the baby to her shoulder, then giving her a light pat on the back. Ana Maria rewarded the effort with a healthy little burp.

"That's it?" Gabriel sputtered. "That's all it was?"

"Just a gas bubble. Babies need a little help getting them out, you know."

"I know that," he snapped, then immediately shook his head impatiently. "Sorry. I've been going crazy worrying about her, and all she needed was a burp. That makes me look pretty stupid, doesn't it?"

Bella laughed. "Not stupid, just inexperienced. And don't take it personally. I think you're a little overwhelmed right now." She really wanted to ask more about his situation, about his wife's death, but it wasn't her place. And she knew from experience that so many questions hurt. People had asked about Rosie, trying to be kind, of course, but the pain had been unbearable. Still was.

"A *little* overwhelmed is right. And I'm sorry I'm always snapping at you. It's just that every time you've caught me so far I've been at my worst."

Something with which she commiserated as she hadn't exactly been at her best lately either. "Believe me, I gave up making assumptions and judgments a long time ago. You're having a bad time right now and I understand completely." She glanced sideways at Ana Maria, who'd gone right to sleep with her head on Bella's shoulder. "I think she's OK," she whispered.

Gabriel stepped forward to take Ana Maria, but Bella shook her head. "I know you told me you didn't need my help, but I think you do. So why don't you go sleep for a few hours, get yourself rested to face all the things you're going to have to take care of tomorrow, and I'll take care of Ana Maria, since I'm wrestling with a bout of insomnia anyway? This will keep me from walking the hall all night."

He studied her for a moment, taking in her pink slippers and moving upward. When he reached her face, a warm smiled flickered across his lips, and for the briefest moment his eyes were so gentle, so...so deep. Then the worry came back, and along with it the scowl he seemed to wear all the time. "I appreciate this, Arabella. It's been rough, and unexpected. From the time I got word that Lynda had died…" He broke off, swallowed hard. "You're right. I do need to sleep. So maybe if I can grab a couple of hours my disposition will improve."

"Your disposition is fine."

"My disposition is lousy, and you're too kind to mention it." He smiled wearily. "But thank you for trying to make me feel better. So, are you sure you don't mind doing this?"

"I don't mind," she said, lowering Ana Maria into her crib. This was what she did after all. She took care of children. That's how she defined herself, the way she felt safe.

"Then I promise I'll be nicer when I wake up." He made a cross-my-heart gesture. "And better with Ana Maria, too."

Bella smiled at Gabriel, but didn't say a word as she settled herself into the chair next to the crib. But she did watch him wander into the bedroom of the suite. He'd be a good father given some time and confidence, she thought. Once he got used to it.

Sleep came fast, and hard. He didn't dream, although he'd thought he would. Didn't have thoughts of his sister to keep him awake. Once he'd slumped into bed, that was it. He was out cold. But not for long. It had been only three hours, and he was awake again. Now he was being bombarded by the thoughts he'd wanted to avoid, the feelings he'd wanted to dismiss.

He was angry, damned angry. Lynda shouldn't have died. She had been young, strong, healthy. Sure, women died in childbirth. But why his sister?

He could have been there, should have been there. Maybe he could have done something, seen something. Gotten his sister to a hospital somewhere.

Pacing over to the window, Gabriel pulled back the heavy curtains and looked outside. The city was dark now. And it seemed so…small. When he had been a boy, Iquitos had been the world. It had had everything. And on those few trips when his parents had brought him here, he'd been exposed to amazing culture and things he hadn't even known existed in this world. But now the city seemed tiny, compared to Chicago. That was home now, and held everything he wanted. Large medical practice, nice condo on the lake, great lifestyle. He couldn't even imagine living in a village like Lado De la

Montaña again, let alone a city such as this. When he had been young, that life had been all he'd known. It was all in his past though, and he couldn't go back. Didn't want to go back. Which meant Ana Maria would be returning to Chicago with him since his mother wasn't physically able to raise a baby and there was no one else. Not even the child's father, Hector.

"Hector doesn't want the child," his mother had told him. "Nor does his other wife, Estella. They have three daughters already and Hector wanted Lynda to give them a son. That's why he married her, to give him the son Estella could not. But since Lynda did not, Hector has refused to take this child in and Estella wants no part of raising another woman's daughter."

It didn't make sense to him. How could a man simply give away his child that way? But that's what had happened. Hector had taken Ana Maria straightway to the village priest, signed the papers giving up custody, and walked away. Probably to find another wife who would might give him that son.

Gabriel had never liked his sister's marriage arrangement. But in the villages it wasn't uncommon for the men to have two wives at once.

Lynda had been Hector Ramirez's second wife, one who'd come into the marriage a good ten years after Hector's first marriage. Oh, he'd tried arguing his sister out of it, but she'd told him that he lived in a different culture now, and his ways were not hers. Hector was a good man, Lynda had contended. He'd make her a good husband.

Yeah, well, what kind of *good* man abandoned his child after the death of the baby's mother?

Gabriel continued staring at the empty street below for another few minutes, trying not to think. But there was a little girl just outside his door he couldn't take his mind off. And a woman tending to her who'd captured a fair share of his thoughts, too. Arabella seemed to be clinging to Ana Maria as if she was a lifeline, what was her story anyway? He thought about asking her, then thought better of it. How could a man who didn't know enough to burp a baby take on another person's problems? The answer was simple—he couldn't.

But he did wonder about Arabella. And worried a little because, come morning, when he and Ana Maria returned to the village, what would she do?

Curiosity got the better of him and, after fifteen minutes of restlessness, Gabriel crept to the bedroom door and peeked out to the sitting area. The room was so quiet he didn't want to disturb either of them. As he started to pull his door to, he heard Arabella whisper, "She's just fine. Sleeping like she should."

Opening the door again, he stepped out, but barely moved past the frame. "Are you OK?" he whispered. "Can I get you anything?" It was an awkward moment between them, the two of them in the near-dark. But what was even more awkward than the moment was the feeling coming over him. It was like…like this was the way it was supposed to be, with Arabella and him watching over the baby. And it was very nice. Disquieting, but pleasant.

Or maybe it was merely an aversion to responsibility, and Arabella presented the easiest solution for the moment. No need to romanticize that, was there? She was good at a task he didn't accept as his own yet. That's what it was. He was simply stalling the inevitable.

Rather than whispering across the room and risk disturbing Ana Maria, Bella came over to Gabriel's door. "I think maybe I should be asking you how you are. With everything you've been through, someone needs to be taking care of you."

"Are you always so…generous? I've taken up your entire day, and now your night, and here you are asking me how I am." She was a woman used to giving, but one, he suspected, who never took. He wondered if she even knew how.

"Trust me, I didn't have much of a day or night planned for myself that having you take it up interrupted anything I wanted to do."

"Why are you here, Arabella?" he asked, even to his own ears sounding much more seductive than he'd intended.

"In your room, or in Peru?"

Ah, she was good at the art of avoidance, too. He was more curious now than he had been but he'd respect her privacy, if that's what she preferred. Grant her the same space she did him. "Look, just so it won't seem like I'm prying, I checked your credentials earlier."

She arched her eyebrows, but didn't say a word.

"I found out you're a very good doctor, in a highly regarded medical practice in California."

"That's all?"

"That's all I needed. Because of Ana Maria."

"You can't be too careful these days, can you?" She smiled, and it was such a soft smile it gave him goose bumps. "And just so you'll know the rest of the story, I've resigned from my practice, which leaves me time to explore different possibilities for my career."

"What kind of possibilities?"

"Honestly, I don't know. I suppose I'll know it when I see it."

More avoidance. He was more curious now than just a moment ago. Apparently there were secrets behind all that sadness in her eyes. So, on that rather obvious cue it was time to shift the conversation. Or let it drop—which he didn't want to do yet. The truth was, he liked talking to Arabella, even if it was more of a one-sided conversation, with him doing most of the conversing. "Do you like Peru?" He asked for a lack of something better to say.

"I hope so."

Odd, again. "This is your first time here?"

Glancing down at the floor, Arabella nodded yet said nothing, leaving Gabriel to wonder even more what it was about Arabella that drew him in. She was so vulnerable, like she needed someone to protect her. Yet she was strong, maybe even a little defiant. So, did she have someone in her life to protect her, someone who saw her needs even more keenly than he believed he was seeing? Did she have someone back in her own room who wondered why she was spending the night in another man's room, or perhaps someone who understood why she was compelled to do it? Because he understood. Even without knowing much about her, what he'd come to understand was that she was totally giving, a woman who couldn't look the other way when she saw need.

Truthfully, he did feel guilty, like he was taking advantage of that. Sure, he'd turned down her offer at the clinic, but when he'd found her at his hotel door there was nothing in him that could have or would have turned her down a second time. He wanted to think it was because he was intrigued by the lady. But his own motives here were suspect, even to him. Or maybe overwhelmed was a better way to describe it. "It's OK that you're here, isn't it?" he asked, sounding like a selfish dolt, as this was the question he should have asked right off. Except he'd been totally preoccupied by his own problems at that moment and hadn't even thought about Arabella other than what she could do to help him. But now he wanted to know. "No one's going to be angry that you're here in my room and not somewhere else…with someone else."

She laughed. "No, I don't have anybody back in my room waiting for me, if that's what you're asking."

"Did it come out that awkwardly? Because I was trying to be subtle."

"Yes, I'm afraid it did. As awkward as anything I've heard in a while."

Gabriel chuckled, then immediately cut if off for fear he would wake Ana Maria. "So, then, how does one go about asking personal questions without being too personal about it? Because I do want to respect your privacy, but I'd also like to satisfy my own curiosity."

"Ask, and I'll answer. Or not."

"OK, are you married?"

"No. Not married, not seriously involved. No children. No future plans in any of those directions. And no more questions on that aspect of my life. So, next question?"

In the dark shadows he could barely make out the brief smile on her lips. Stunning. Lips he would have kissed under different circumstances…a thought that caused him to take a step back. "Would you rather have the bed?" he asked, awkwardly again, then clarified it. "Alone."

"Under the circumstances, I think you need it

more than I do. I'm fine in the chair." She took a step backward, too. "And I think we should be quiet now. I don't want Ana Maria to wake up." She took another step, and turned around. But before she returned to the chair by the crib she turned back to Gabriel, studied him for a moment, then smiled. "Thank you for letting me do this. It makes things better for a little while."

Better? He wanted to ask what was better, but he didn't. With all the mixed-up feelings rushing through him just now, he was safer not knowing.

"Damn," he muttered, as he dropped back down into bed. There were too many complications, and he hated complications. All he wanted was to go back a few days in time, to when Lynda had been alive and happy about her pregnancy, when his life had been just the way he'd planned it. When he hadn't even known Dr. Arabella Burke existed.

Well, maybe that's the one thing he *would* have changed in all this confusion—meeting Arabella. He was glad he had because she was interesting. Outside her obvious physical attributes, and she'd been blessed with more than her fair share, she was smart, compassionate, dedicated. But her sad eyes bothered him, much more than they should have. Much more than he wanted to allow, but he really didn't have any control over that. Even as he drifted off to sleep again, that's the image that stayed with him—those sad, sad eyes.

"She's doing well this morning?" Gabriel asked. He wandered over to the crib and looked down, only to find Ana Maria looking up at him. It was hard looking at her, remembering all his sister's plans. She'd been so excited when she'd called him with the news of her pregnancy, and every time they'd talked after that she'd been so full of expectation, talking about having more babies, saying how good she felt even though her belly was big and her ankles were swollen. So he still had a difficult time looking at the baby because there was always such an overflow of bitter-sweet memories. "No more upset stomach?" he asked, trying to sound clinical about it.

"She had a very good night. Slept like she should have. I think she'd probably like some-thing a little more substantial than the sugar water in her stomach this morning."

"Well, I'm on my way down to the front desk to pick up the formula. Señora Hernandez, from the clinic, rang me up a few minutes ago, and she's waiting downstairs. So, do you mind staying here a little longer?" The truth was, the logistics of handling a baby and doing everything else that needed to be done befuddled him. He'd told the nurse he'd be right down before he'd even considered that he would have to deal with Ana Maria somewhere in that arrangement, too. And carting a baby around while he tried moving several cases of formula wasn't practical. But he wasn't disposed to planning ahead the way he needed to now. Wasn't even in the frame of mind to think of it yet.

It ever there was someone who wasn't cut out to raise a child…

"We'll be just fine here," Bella said. "Take all the time you need. And I think I'll give Ana Maria a bath. Do you have any clean clothes for her?"

Clean clothes? He'd picked up diapers yesterday, but of all the stupid things he hadn't thought about clothes! "I, um… No clothes."

Bella laughed. "We'll make something work. Don't worry about it."

But he had to worry. That was the problem. There were so many things to worry about now, even if he didn't know what they were. "This won't take long, then I'll go out and buy some clothes. Um…would you mind making me a list of other things you think she'll need?"

"Sure, I'll have it ready when you bring the formula back to the room. And don't worry about how long it takes. I don't exactly have a set schedule here, so my time is whatever I want to make of it, and right now this is what I want to make of it."

"In case I didn't mention this before, you're too good," he said, hurrying out the door. Waiting at the elevator, he tried concentrating on his mental task list, but Arabella kept distracting him. He didn't really date much, and he didn't date for long because he hated getting out of commitments, and anything more than two or three dates turned into a commitment. But he was doing well in his practice, loving the lifestyle and not in a particular hurry to change it. Still, with Arabella he saw permanence and commitment, which should have scared him to death. Yet it didn't, and all he could do was think that when his life settled down again, he might look her up. The distance from Chicago to San Francisco wasn't that far, after all.

More evidence of crazy, mixed-up emotions,

he decided. His life was suddenly out of control and, subconsciously, Arabella presented a good solution. Jumping too far ahead of himself the way he was didn't mean anything more than a little panic attack. In a life that now had to be lived from moment to moment until he could figure out the best way to manage all parts of it, there were no future plans other than getting through the day. Especially future plans that included permanence and commitment.

But honey-colored hair and green eyes certainly attracted him like he hadn't been attracted in a while…like he'd never been attracted before, actually, and that had nothing to do with plans or futures or babies or anything else. And for the life of him it didn't seem all that crazy and mixed up, which proved just how crazy and mixed up it really was.

So, who was this stranger who'd stepped into his life and become so important in what had taken no longer than the blink of an eye? Apart from what he'd been told about her medical qualifications, who was Arabella Burke?

"Dr. Velascos," Nurse Hernandez said, extending her thin hand to him. "I'm assuming you know what this is about, that Melaina Juarez suggested our meeting?" She also extended a thin, nervous smile. Señora Hernandez was older, probably close to his mother's age, with black and gray-streaked hair pulled back into a tight knot, and she wore a starchy white uniform like he rarely saw on nurses these days.

Gabriel took her hand and noted her firm shake. Judging by her grip, she was a woman who meant business. Judging from the tight expression on her face, she was well ready to get on with it. "I was aware that they were helping with the arrangements, yes. And thank you for coming, Señora Hernandez. Although you didn't have to bother. I'd have been happy coming to you."

She cocked her head slightly to the left, frowning. "That's not necessary, Doctor. Considering the circumstances of the arrangements we usually make, it's our aim to make this transition as easy as possible on you."

Something was wrong here, and he didn't like the way the warning hairs were standing up on the back of his neck. "What are we talking about, Señora Hernandez? The baby formula?"

"Not formula, Doctor. The adoption of your niece. Melaina Juarez informed us that you're involved in a very difficult situation over your sister's death, and that you might be agreeable with allowing us to find a proper home for the child. Ana Maria is her name, I believe?"

Gabriel took a step backward, opened his mouth to speak, then closed it again for several seconds before he tried, once more, to speak. "What the hell are you talking about?" he sputtered. "I never indicated to anyone that I wanted someone to adopt my niece!"

"But didn't you tell Nurse Juarez how you never expected to have a baby in your life, and that you didn't know what to do? Melaina indicated that you didn't want the child."

Had it seemed like that? Yesterday was such a blur he couldn't remember. But there had been conversation while Ana Maria had been under observation for those few hours, and maybe something he'd said had been misinterpreted. Or perhaps he'd been overcome by the whole emotional roller-coaster, and saying something he hadn't meant. "You're correct. I didn't expect to have a child, and no, I'm not thrilled about making the change in my life that will be necessary, but you're mistaken if you think I'd give away my sister's baby. Because I won't!"

"I know this is a trying time for you, Doctor. But let me make it clear what we do. We place children in good, loving homes where children are wanted. Our waiting lists are long, our clients worthy and we do an extensive search of their backgrounds. For people such as yourself, it's an ideal situation." She handed him a packet of information. "I'd like you to consider what we have to offer your niece. Getting her into a nice, stable family situation where she's wanted, and doing it at such a young age, is to her benefit. So, please, just read the brochures, and I'll contact you in a day or two."

"I'm not letting anybody take Ana Maria!" Adoption wasn't a solution he'd considered, wasn't even a solution he liked. Not for his flesh and blood. But if worse came to worst? Could he turn over Lynda's child?

Not a chance in hell! That answer came to him in a fraction of a second, which surprised him because he hadn't realized his feelings were so strong. But they were. Something else would work out, but it would have nothing to do with giving Ana Maria to strangers. Even the thought of that made him sick to his stomach. "Look, I appreciate your coming here like this, Señora Hernandez, but I don't think…"

She laid a comforting hand on his forearm. "It's too early to *think*, Dr. Velascos. That's why we urge our prospective clients to take all the time they need. It's a serious situation, giving up a child, and we certainly don't want anyone making a decision they'll later regret. So, please, just read the information. That's all I'm asking you to do right now."

Gabriel drew in a sharp breath. Too much, too soon. He wasn't prepared to deal with any of this yet. "I know you're only doing your job, but I'm not going to have anyone adopt my niece. Whatever Melaina Juarez might have thought I meant was incorrect, and I'm sorry for any inconvenience I've caused. I was under stress and I may have said some things that were mistaken as an intention to give away the baby, but that's certainly not what I'm going to do." It seemed abominable, but there was no need being brutal to the woman.

"It's never easy, Dr. Velascos. But think about what's best for Ana Maria." She stepped back. "I have appointments in a few of the villages near Lado De la Montaña over the next few days, so I'll be back in touch with you in due course."

He didn't say yes, he didn't say no. And maybe

he should have. But the image running through his mind as Señora Hernandez walked away from him was one where she was taking Ana Maria with her, and that caused such a sudden and unexpected pain in his gut he couldn't speak. Couldn't utter a single word.

"Breakfast?"

Bella nodded. "I called room service. But since I didn't know what you'd like, I had them bring several different things."

He looked at the cart full of sweet rolls and various juices and tea, but he just didn't have the stomach to eat any of it.

"And they brought up the formula, too."

She pointed to where the stack of cases was sitting next to the door, but he was more interested in watching the way she stood at the window, rocking Ana Maria back in forth in her arms—the perfect picture of motherhood. It made him sad, and angry all over again. Not at her, but at…everything. And the baby formula was just another reminder of how his life was changing in ways he couldn't control. "I don't know what I would have done without you, Arabella, but I can't keep depending on you the way I've been doing. We've taken up too much of your time."

"I have nothing *but* time. And I thought you wanted to go buy some baby clothes."

He looked at the way she'd tied Ana Maria into one of his T-shirts. There were so many things he needed to do, and shopping for baby clothes was only one of them. "We'll manage." Easy to say, but not easy to do.

"Why don't I stay here for a little while longer? Taking care of Ana Maria makes me feel like I'm back in my element, and I've needed that."

Under the circumstances, the best he could do was offer Bella a stiff nod. Now that the formula was here, it was suddenly all about the days ahead of him. He was on the brink of raising a child. There was nothing to put off any longer. *This was his new reality, his new life, and he was drowning in it.*

"Go run your errands, Gabriel," she said gently. "I think it's all catching up with you and maybe getting out for a little while, taking a walk, clearing your head, will do you some good." She handed him the list. "I called the front desk and was told there's a little mercantile two blocks over that will have everything Ana Maria needs."

"You always think of everything, don't you?" Another time, another place, she could have been the one to change his mind about so many things. "Look, Arabella, I appreciate this more than you can know. It's all too new to me. Nothing I'd planned for, nothing that I'd really wanted at this point in my life, nothing that really fits into my lifestyle, and it's going to take some getting used to." He pulled the adoption agency papers from his pocket, crumpled them and tossed them at the trash can next to the door. Then he stepped forward. "This won't take me long."

"Go do your errands, Gabriel. Take all the time you need. We'll be just fine here."

"Thank you," he said, reaching out to brush her cheek. He wanted to touch her, to feel the softness of her skin, but he caught himself in time and pulled back. Then Gabriel walked out the door, shut it firmly behind him, took five steps toward the elevator, and slumped against the hall wall, breaking out in a profuse sweat. Shaking hands, tight chest, wobbly knees, sagging shoulders…it was all finally beginning to sink in. This was happening to him. *Really happening to him.*

* * *

As if on cue, the baby started crying the split second Gabriel closed the door, to which Bella responded by pacing back and forth across the room, cuddling and rocking her. "It's going to be just fine," she reassured the infant. "Your daddy will get over his jitters and the two of you will get along just fine. I know it's tough not having a mother. I didn't have one for very long. But you'll have a good life with your daddy as soon as he calms down." Was Gabriel a man who'd counted on his wife doing all the parenting? Was that why he was such an emotional mess when it came to the baby? Or perhaps he hadn't wanted a child at all. He'd said something about not planning on this? So maybe there'd been problems with his wife over her pregnancy then, when she'd died, the remorse over it had set in. They could have argued the way she and Rosie had argued that last time…

That was a bitter guilt she understood very well.

She'd done everything but cope with her sister's death these past weeks and, even now, when she was on the verge of coming face-to-face with the hardest thing she'd ever had to do in her life, she was avoiding it every way she could. Including getting involved with Gabriel and Ana Maria. That's why she recognized that Gabriel was avoiding the inevitable right now, because she was the expert at it, a virtual master of pretexts and avoidance.

"It's not easy, forcing yourself to do something you don't want to do," she said to the baby. Did he love his baby? Maybe he blamed for her mother's death? "I know you don't understand what I'm saying, but be patient with your father. He's dealing with a tragedy no one's ever prepared for. When you lose someone like he has…like I did…you lose part of yourself, too. Then it becomes so hard getting up in the morning to face the normal things you're supposed to. People stare at you and whisper, they pity you and they mean to be kind, but it hurts so much and you have to put on this brave face and pretend that you're doing well when everything inside you wants to crumble. You don't know what to do, yet life has to go on even when it doesn't make as much sense as it used to." She sighed. "So that's why you have to be patient with him. Your daddy's starting over again, and his footing isn't very sure yet." Like hers wasn't. But something about holding Ana Maria made it seem better. Maybe it was because she already missed her medical practice, missed the one solid thing in her life that had never let her down, *other than her sister*, and Ana Maria reminded her of that stability. "You just wait. It will get better gradually, and pretty soon neither of you will remember the first few clumsy days."

Pacing over to the door, Bella was about to turn and pace back to the window when she glanced down at the papers Gabriel had tossed at the trash can and missed. After she'd bent to pick them up, it had been her intention to throw them away, but what she saw caused her to pull Ana Maria to her chest even more. It was an adoption pamphlet. No! That couldn't be right. Gabriel couldn't be… Was he actually thinking about giving up his child for adoption? Giving away his baby and start over? "No," she gasped, throwing the adoption information in the trash. She'd thought his detachment would disappear once he was over the shock. It was too soon to make this kind of decision—too soon, too reactionary. But she'd been wrong about Gabriel, and this went far beyond not thinking clearly.

She looked at the trash can, wanting to kick it she was so angry. Those brochures were crumpled and intended for the trash, weren't they? Could he have considered the idea, then changed his mind?

Or maybe he'd already signed the adoption papers and didn't need the information brochures any longer. It was a thought that turned her stomach.

"Gabriel," she whispered, the full weight of a sadness she didn't even grasp dropping down on her as she dragged her way back to the window. It was such a beautiful sight out there, with the neatly manicured gardens below. Beautiful green grass, perfectly sculpted shrubs lining the walkways, flower-beds all done in reds and whites, white wicker benches on the lawn. All of it made so much sense. Went together the way it should. But glancing down at Ana Maria, who'd settled into her arms to nap, she couldn't find any sense in what she feared Gabriel was about to do. No sense at all.

Just like there was no sense in the way she was feeling over it—betrayed.

"You didn't touch the pastries you ordered," Gabriel commented casually an hour later. Entering the hotel room, he wasn't bogged down by the bundle of packages she'd hoped he might be bringing. Packages full of baby clothes would mean he wasn't going to give Ana Maria away. But all he had with him was a small bag with a couple of new sleepers in it. Nothing else, and she'd had so many things on her list—receiving blankets, newborn soaps and lotions, bootees. Which only served to refuel all the raw emotions she'd been feeling from the moment she'd found his adoption literature.

No, she wouldn't do this. Wouldn't get involved. It was none of her business and she meant to keep it that way. She had her own problems to fix, her own hard decisions to make, and getting involved in his life in any way was just crazy.

Sucking in a sharp breath, Bella squared her shoulders, marched past Gabriel and straight out the door, without so much as a glance backward or a goodbye. Tears welled in her eyes all the way from his room to hers, and she fought them back, biting hard on her lower lip, hoping the pain would distract her emotions.

But it didn't. Back in her own room, of all the things to do over a stranger, she collapsed on her bed, drew herself up in a ball and cried like she hadn't cried since the day she'd heard about the airplane crash. She had no right to those tears, neither did she understand them, yet once they started they didn't stop for nearly an hour. And at the end, when her eyes were all puffy and red, her face blotched, and she was dabbing cold water on herself, she glanced at the distorted face in the mirror, wondering who'd she been crying for. Her sister? Ana Maria? Gabriel?

Or her own broken heart over so many things she knew and possibly some she didn't?

Bella searched her own eyes for a moment, then bent low over the vanity sink and splashed more cold water on her face. Better that than finding the answer she was afraid she'd discover if she kept on looking.

CHAPTER THREE

BELLA glanced at the map, then at the road ahead of her. This wasn't what she'd bargained for. Rutted pits that passed for roads, a rental car that just barely passed for a car, a map that was more of an artist's impression than a factual interpretation of the topography—it should have been easier. That's all there was to it. Her trip to Lado De la Montaña simply shouldn't have been this difficult. But she was four hours into what should have been a two-hour journey now, her back ached from all the bumps, her head ached from the frustration of the situation she'd put herself into, and on top of all that she couldn't get her mind off Gabriel and his daughter. What he was going to do bothered her, no matter if he actually intended on going through with it or was merely thinking about it. Either way, it made her angry.

She did know where to contact him—through

his Chicago office, at the hotel, through Dr. Navarro, and she'd picked up the phone a dozen times to do that, to ask him to take some time to rethink his decision. Each time, though, she'd had second and third thoughts about getting involved in his life, especially now, at a time when her life was on the verge of some drastic changes.

She'd come here to see about setting up the clinic Rosie had wanted to set up, and that had to be her single focus. Rosie had loved this area when she'd first come here with a traveling medical company a couple of years before. After that her heart had been set on returning. And she'd almost got here... She *was* here, somewhere. But the plane wreckage had never been found. Nurse Rosie Burke and three other medics had perished somewhere in the Andes and now Bella was here to...to, well, she wasn't sure why yet. She told herself it was to see about setting up Rosie's clinic, and that had been the motivation that had finally gotten her here.

"I should have hired a guide," she muttered, wadding up her map and throwing it into the car. Backing up to lean against the driver's door, Bella raised her hand to visor her eyes and squinted up at the mountain looming ahead of her. As mountains went, it was impressive. Beautiful. Lush green. Alive. And so frightening. Another thing to avoid.

Sighing, she took a drink from the bottle of water she grasped in her hand then turned to open her car door just as a battered old truck wheezed its way round the curve and nearly swerved into the back fender of her rental. Its driver threw on the brakes and hit the horn at the same time as the truck fishtailed all over the dirt road and finally came to a stop on the opposite side in the grass.

Bella's first reaction was anger over what had almost happened, but her second was concern for the people in the truck, which propelled her across the road and straight to the driver's side. "Gabriel?" she sputtered, pulling open the truck door at the same time he tried shoving it out.

"What the hell?"

"You almost hit me," Bella shouted, on her way round to the passenger's side.

"You were sitting in the middle of the road. Didn't it ever occur to you that someone could come around the curve and run into you?"

"I was pulled off to the side. There was plenty of room to get around me if you were paying attention."

"You were pulled off in a spot with absolutely no visibility from where I was coming."

"On the shoulder. There was no place else to stop." She reached for the baby the same time Gabriel did, but she didn't give way to him. Instead, she took Ana Maria out of the child carrier and did a quick check. She looked good. The little jostle hadn't upset her. In fact, the instant Ana Maria settled into Bella's arms, she went straight to sleep like that was where she was meant to be.

"She's OK?" Gabriel asked, climbing across the seat, then getting out.

"Perfect, no thanks to the way you were driving. What were you thinking?"

"What I was thinking was that nobody would be stupid enough to stop along this road."

Granted, it was narrow. The visibility wasn't so good either. But coming up from behind her, Gabriel had had plenty of time to see her and stop, which made her wonder where his attention had been fixed. On the baby? Or on his wife?

Or maybe on the adoption agency he was going to give Ana Maria to? No! It wasn't any of her business. She had to keep reminding herself that she wasn't involved in this. "Ana Maria's not hurt, and the rest of it doesn't matter, OK?"

"Except you could have gotten us all hurt. Or killed."

"I wasn't the one *not* paying attention, Gabriel. I don't know what you had your mind on, and I really don't care, but you're the one who nearly ran into me, not the other way around. So don't go blaming me, and don't take out whatever hostility you've got going on me either."

"Hostility? You're calling me hostile after the way you stormed out of my hotel room this morning?"

That much was true. She had. And even now, thinking about what he wanted to do with his baby brought her blood right back to a boil. "Look, I don't want to argue with you, Gabriel. In fact, I don't want to have anything to do with you. I know you've gone through a lot these past few days...more than most people could cope with. And I'm sorry for that. But I didn't come to Peru to deal with...with people like you. We all face situations the best way we know how, and I understand that. But what you're doing... Look, instead of standing here on the side of the road, fighting about something that's none of my business in the first place, if you'll just head me off in the direction of Lado De la Montaña, we can both get back into our vehicles and go our separate ways." That seemed reasonable enough. A clean parting. She would do what she'd come here to do and Gabriel would… No, she didn't want to think about what he would do.

Bella stepped forward to hand Ana Maria back to Gabriel, but he didn't take her right away. Rather, he squared his shoulders like he was about to square off with her. "That's not possible," he said, as a tiny smile crept to his lips.

He thought this was funny? Apparently Dr. Gabriel Velascos wasn't all the man she'd considered him to be. "What's not possible?"

"Separate ways. Not possible."

"Why not?"

"Because I'm going to Lado De la Montaña, too."

Bella opened her mouth to speak, but shut it again. This couldn't be happening. Just couldn't be. Of all the inconceivable coincidences, how was it that this man seemed to be everywhere she was? The clinic, the hotel, the tiny mountain village near where her sister had been killed.

"Why? Are you following me? Is that what this is about, Gabriel? You saw the connection I made with Ana Maria and now you're thinking that maybe I'll be the one to take her off your hands?" The words poured out before she thought about what she was saying, but she didn't regret them. Maybe what she'd said was right. Gabriel could have seen her as the solution to his little problem and followed her, hoping she'd be the one to adopt his daughter. For that matter, what was to keep him from getting in his truck right now and driving away, leaving her here with the baby?

"What are you talking about?"

"Giving up your daughter for adoption. I saw the papers from the agency, Gabriel. And after you told me you didn't want her…"

"My daughter?" He glanced down at Ana Maria briefly, then shook his head. "She's not my daughter, Bella. Didn't Dr. Navarro tell you?"

"Tell me what?"

"Ana Maria is my sister's daughter. Lynda died in childbirth and the child was given to my mother, who can't care for her."

"Which is why you're so quick to give her up for adoption. Now I understand."

"You don't understand anything! I never said I didn't want her. I said I'd never planned on having a child, that she didn't fit into my life. But that doesn't mean I don't want her, and it sure as hell doesn't mean I'm going to give her away."

"Then what about the adoption brochures?"

"The nurse in Raul Navarro's office thought it might be a solution for me. That's all. When Señora Hernandez from the adoption agency came to the hotel this morning I told her that I wouldn't even consider giving away my sister's child."

"You said you were going to go buy several things for Ana Maria, and when you returned you had almost nothing. A baby who's going to be adopted doesn't require much."

"So you thought that because I didn't buy all kinds of little frilly dresses and baby toys, I was giving her away?" Gabriel huffed out a perturbed sigh. "That's why you left the way you did, isn't it? Before I could thank you, before you could say goodbye to Ana Maria. You just assumed that I was giving her up because you saw the pamphlets, and because I didn't return with bundles of baby things…which I'd left in the truck, by the way."

"So you're not…" she started, then stopped, feeling more sheepish now than anything else.

"Look, I'll be the first one to admit that I don't know how the hell I'm going to take care of a newborn, or a toddler, little girl or teenager, but giving her up… No! I couldn't do that. It's the easiest thing to do probably, but it's not right." Impulsively, he reached over and brushed a strand of hair from her cheek. "Thank you for caring so strongly, Arabella. For my sake, but especially for Ana Maria's. She's already lost her mother and father, and while I'm not sure what I'm going to do beyond keeping her and raising her…"

"Her father, too?" Like she and Rosie had, when they'd been so young.

Gabriel nodded. "My sister was a second wife, the one who was supposed to bear her husband the son his first wife hadn't been able to give him. When Lynda died, her husband didn't want another daughter to feed and his wife didn't want to raise another woman's daughter so they simply gave the baby to the priest, who takes care of matters like this. The father's idea of taking care of matters was giving the baby to her family… in this case my mother, who gave her to me.

Adoption is an easy solution for some, but not for me, and I suppose that's where you got the idea that I wouldn't keep her." He paused for a moment, as if choosing his next words carefully, before he continued. "I'm not going so far as to say I want to raise a baby at this point in my life because the truth is, it scares me to death. You've seen how clueless I am at it, and I'll be the first one to admit that. But I'd never give her away to strangers because she is my sister's daughter, and my sister was so excited to be having her. It's about family. And Ana Maria deserves better than being tossed aside by her family."

"I think she already has better, Gabriel."

"Well, that remains to be seen, doesn't it? I'm still hoping her father will change his mind after he's gotten over the initial shock of losing his wife. He's not a bad man. Just a practical one, in terms of his own life, I suppose."

"Practical," Bella repeated. She and Rosie had lived a "practical" life with their guardian… practical in terms of the caregivers he'd hired to look after them, practical in terms of the boarding schools he'd finally sent them to. But a child's own father giving her to the village priest because he didn't want her? She didn't consider that kind of abandonment practical in any terms. More like heartless.

"It's a different world here, Arabella. To some, a house full of daughters doesn't have the same worth as a house full of sons. Hector's part of that tradition and he wanted that son. He probably learned it from the time he could walk, and I'm not sure what, if anything, could force him to change."

"But you're from here, and you're not that way."

"I live in Chicago. And have done for a long time, and my ways have changed since I left here. If I'd stayed, and never been introduced to different standards, who knows? I could have been just like my sister's husband, wanting a boy, not interested in another girl." He finally took Ana Maria from Bella's arms, stared at her for a moment, then smiled. Only for an instant, though.

Relief, pure and simple, washed down over her for many reasons. First, and foremost, was Ana Maria's future. It wasn't so uncertain now. All those bad things she'd thought about Gabriel weren't true. That was a relief, but the biggest relief was what she'd just seen in the tender way he'd looked at the child. "I don't think you could be like that, Gabriel. The customs here might be different, but a person's values…those don't change no matter where that person lives. You wouldn't have given away your daughter no matter what. And I owe you an apology for jumping to so many wrong conclusions."

"No apology necessary. You were only thinking of Ana Maria, and that was nice. So tell me, why are you going to Lado De la Montaña? It's not exactly a thriving center of tourism."

"I'm thinking about opening a medical clinic there," she said, offering no further explanation about her sister. "Or somewhere nearby."

He blinked his surprise. "Why would the doctor from San Francisco give up her life there to come here?"

"For the same reason the doctor from Lado De la Montaña would give up his life here to go to Chicago. Changes, I suppose. You sought yours one way and I'm seeking mine another. And it's not definite, so I'd appreciate you not saying anything to the people there until I've made my decision. I don't want them counting on something then being disappointed if I change my mind." God forbid she should cause more disappointment than she already had. "So now I need to get to Lado De la Montaña."

"But you're not going to tell me why you want to do this?"

"It looked lovely in the travel brochures," she lied. "A nice place to settle down." He was suffering over the death of his sister, and he'd gotten here in such a quick time after the tragedy. What would he think about her if he knew that her sister had died here a couple of months ago, and she hadn't come at all? Hadn't come to stand watch with the other families, in hopes that the bodies would be discovered and returned. Hadn't come to the memorial service held in the little church in the village? Or hadn't placed a tombstone on an empty grave when the wreckage was never found, like the other families had done. She wasn't proud of all that, but she'd shut down after she'd received word. That's all there was to say. She'd shut down physically and emotionally, and wasn't all that far past it even now. So how could someone like Gabriel, who did the right things when they were so difficult for him, ever understand? It was simple. He wouldn't. So she'd never tell him, which was another of her easy avoidances.

"Well, I'm sure you'll tell me in your own good time," he said, taking Ana Maria from her arms. "Especially since it seems we'll be bumping into each other for a while longer."

They crept along the winding dirt road at a snail's pace for nearly an hour, Gabriel in the lead, his truck kicking dust all over her car as Bella followed a respectable distance behind him. He was being overly cautious in his speed, with Ana Maria on board, and she liked that. Gabriel might not be a father in the sense she'd first thought him to be, but the emotional bond was beginning to form. She was glad to see it in the way he looked at his niece when he thought nobody would notice, and the fact that a doctor from Chicago was facing a baby crisis in Peru, and not taking the easy way out in doing it, was quite telling.

That pleased her about Gabriel. In fact, Gabriel pleased her in many ways. Too many ways. She was going to have to be careful about that. Especially if she decided to take a different course with her life. Gabriel wouldn't live here again. And the odds were she would stay.

Still, it was amazing how two different people suffering such similar tragedies had come together like they had. If she'd been a big believer in the Fates, or destiny, or whatever it was in the universe that created such parallel circumstances, she might had admitted there could be a purpose in bringing together two people who'd come to the same place to reconcile themselves with two tragedies so alike it was almost uncanny. But it was easier, and more practical, attributing it to mere coincidence, then let it go at that. No more thinking about it, no more trying to draw comparisons. Anything else would put Gabriel and herself together in a way she didn't want to be put. *Not with anyone.* Especially *not* with someone like Dr. Gabriel Velascos, who'd lost his heart to a different way of life than what she was about to undertake. Keep it easy, keep her distance. Hide her heart because it couldn't take another break.

Sighing, Bella set her rental car in Park as they finally reached the village and Gabriel drove on down the road, then she stepped out, not sure what came next at this point in her journey. She was here and she wanted to be, yet she didn't want to be. This was her destination, though, one of the several villages said to be close to where her sister's plane most likely had gone down. Nobody knew for sure, since the wreckage was never discovered, but the aviation experts were fairly certain this was the general area, and Rosie had specifically mentioned Lado De la Montaña as one of the places she would consider for a permanent clinic because it was central to so many other areas. Also, the landing strip they were to have used was only twenty kilometers away.

"I don't feel you yet," she whispered. "I wanted to, but I don't feel you here." For some strange reason she'd thought she'd feel her sister when she got here. Or maybe that's what she'd wanted. But even as she shut her eyes and blocked out everything, there were no feelings. *Nothing* overwhelming her, nothing even very sad. Nothing. She couldn't even cry, which was so strange because she'd thought she'd cry forever once she was finally here. But no tears. "I don't know how to do this, Rosie. You would have, though, wouldn't you? You were the one who knew what to do in every situation and I wish I had some of that in me now. But I don't, and I don't know how to get through this without you."

Bella stood there a good five minutes, eyes shut, listening to the quiet surrounding her, trying to picture her sister, trying to remember her voice, remember the parts of their lives together that had been good, but nothing came to her. She was blank, shut off. And the harder she tried to force herself to a place where she could open up to the feelings she wanted flooding in, the more she pushed them away. Further and further away until she opened her eyes and kicked the rental car's tire just so she could feel the pain...feel anything.

"You are Dr. Burke?" a quiet voice asked from the behind of the car. His accent was heavy, but he spoke English quite well, and she recognized his voice from so many relayed phone calls. A voice that had been her lifeline after the plane crash.

How long had he stood there watching her? Long enough to sense that she was so empty? It didn't matter, really, what he sensed. He was the priest. If anybody could understand a wounded soul, he would. "I didn't hear you, Father," she said, moving her left foot in a circle, hoping to abate the pain she'd just caused herself. "And, yes, I'm Dr. Burke." She might have extended a hand to him, but he took care to keep his distance. In fact, nothing about his demeanor was intrusive as he smiled at her.

"It's nice to finally meet you, Doctor. After talking with you so often it feels like we've already met."

Father Carlos was a diminutive man, garbed in traditional black pants and a black shirt with white clerical collar. Not young, not old, he seemed more…ageless with his salt-and-pepper hair and his kind brown eyes. "It's nice to finally meet you too, Father. And I'm sorry for the delay. I know you expected me yesterday, but…"

"No apologies, Doctor. This is a difficult journey for you. Something you should do in your own way, in your own time."

Did he wonder why she'd never come here before? So many of the other families had said things to her, and about her. Harsh things… things she would never forget. They'd called her selfish and unfeeling, said didn't care about her sister, that she was too busy to bother. They'd said the clinic was Rosie's idea and that, as Rosie's sister, it was her responsibility to stand with the others who were grieving their losses. So, had Father Carlos thought those same things? "I appreciate your kindness," she replied stiffly. "For helping me make the arrangements now, and…and for everything you did back then." Including delivering the eulogy over her sister, one she'd never heard.

"Well, concerning your arrangements now, I'm afraid I'll have to take back my offer of a house for you to stay in. It seems the son of the woman who would have given you a room has come home under some very difficult circumstances…a family tragedy."

"Gabriel?" she asked. "Gabriel Velascos?"

"You know Juan Gabriel?" He arched a speculative eyebrow.

"Yes. We've met—in Iquitos. He was there with Ana Maria and I was there being treated for an ear infection. We were staying at the same hotel—in fact, I followed him here when I got lost."

"Good. Then you understand the situation. It's very sad, the loss of someone you love, as you well know. So you recognize why it's important that he and his mother have their privacy at a time like this. But don't worry. I have a room for you in the church. It's not as comfortable as staying with Gloria Elena would have been, but you'll have a bed and a place to bathe. Several of the villagers have agreed to see to your meals, and you'll find a list of them on the table in your room. We don't often get visitors, so the people here are more than happy to be hospitable."

"I look forward to meeting them."

"Most will speak some English, to make it easier for you. And the children do learn English in the school, so they can interpret, if you need assistance."

"I speak some Spanish," she said. Not as much as Rosie had, but Rosie had prepared herself for a life here. It's all she'd talked about, and worked toward, for a whole year before she'd stepped onto that plane. And now here she was, Rosie's little sister who had a barely passable command of the language, and no preparation whatsoever, thinking she could make it work. It was crazy. *She was crazy.* But she wanted to do this for Rosie.

"Good. Now, the church is at the other end of the road. It's the white wooden structure on the left. Nothing like the churches you're used to, I'm sure, but the door is open and the room is in the back. The sheets are clean, and there's a fresh pitcher of water by the bed. I'm afraid that's all I can offer in the way of conveniences."

"I'm not taking your room, am I?" It suddenly occurred to her that she might be displacing the priest. In which case, she'd find something else. Sleep in the car. Go home.

"No, this is the room we keep ready for poor, wayfaring strangers. I live in the house adjacent to the church."

Now she was a poor, wayfaring stranger? That just seemed to fit her, didn't it? She'd become someone without an aim, someone who wanted no better than to be a stranger. The wayfaring stranger's room would be perfect for her, and five minutes later, after Father Carlos excused himself to go tend to one of the villagers, she saw that it was. No larger than the size of her walk-in closet at home, it was dark, there was no adornment except the bed with a hand-carved crucifix hanging above it, a tiny bedside table, and a small, two-drawer dresser for her clothes. All of it was rough hewn of dark wood, as were the walls and the floor. Yes, this was the perfect place for some self-abasement. Father Carlos couldn't have made better arrangements for her.

"Father Carlos said you have a meal schedule, and that I'm not to distract you," Gabriel said, as Bella stepped out the church door. He'd tracked her down to her little hideaway soon after he'd delivered Ana Maria to his mother's house. "But would you like an escort to Conchata Escabar's house? I understand she's next on your list, and I thought you might need an interpreter."

"It's across the street." Bella pointed to the tiny wooden structure all of twenty paces ahead of her. "I have a detailed map with my list."

"He's very precise. Nice man, good priest, but a taskmaster."

In spite of her glum mood, she laughed. "We all need some of that occasionally, don't we? The benevolent guidance of someone with a rather firm hand in case we don't accept that benevolence."

"Spoken like someone who's done her fair share of avoiding the offered benevolence."

"Not avoiding it so much as trying not to find myself in a position to need it. It's much easier not having to rely on the kindness of strangers, or even friends, for that matter. Self-sufficiency is a good thing, really."

"Again, spoken like someone who's done her fair share of avoiding benevolence."

"Maybe so."

"But my offer to escort you isn't benevolent.

And neither is being your interpreter since Señora Escabar doesn't speak English. She does, however, make the best fish stew on this side of the mountain, and I was hoping that if I showed up on her doorstep she'd take pity on me."

"Ulterior motives don't become you, Doctor. But I can't stop you from walking across the street with me, can I?" Actually, she was a little flattered. It was inevitable that she and Gabriel would bump into each other in a place this size, but in some small way she was pleased that he'd found her so quickly. Of course, ulterior motives did come into it, too. He wanted to know about her—he'd already learned on his own that she was connected to the medical team lost in the crash a couple of months before. The crash that had claimed the life of her sister—but Gabriel didn't yet know that about her. By now he'd heard bits and pieces of why she was here and he wanted more. Everybody would. That's how it would be, and she had to get used to that if she intended on staying. Or else she'd have to make her peace then get out of here as fast as she could. As nice as these people were…benevolent strangers…she didn't want to be bothered by them yet. Didn't want their pity, or their wary stares. Didn't want anything until she knew, for sure, which way her life was headed.

Didn't even want Conchata Escabar's fish stew, which, as it turned out, was wonderful. As was the conversation, most of it which she could not understand. But it was spirited, and when Gabriel wasn't eating, he was translating. Throughout the entire time she was there, Señora Escabar fussed, filled and refilled bowls, heaped warm tortillas on plates, all of which transcended language barriers. And Gabriel did look sufficiently uncomfortable each of the fifteen or so times Señora Escabar pulled him to her ample bosom and nearly squeezed the breath out of him. It was over his sister, Bella realized as the woman squeezed, then wept. But Gabriel was gracious about it, and gracious about taking the kettle of stew with him when they finally left Señora Escabar's house after an hour that didn't turn out nearly as badly as Bella had anticipated.

"She loved my sister," Gabriel explained, as they walked across the road. "She's having a hard time—" He stopped abruptly. "Look, I'm sorry for your loss, Arabella. I know you were part of that medical group…"

"Yes, I was and I wasn't," she said, offering no

more. She would have preferred keeping this relationship with Gabriel on a different level for a while longer but it had just changed. Now they were merely two people suffering from their losses, and because he did it the way it should be done, it would contrast harshly against the way it shouldn't be done. Which, in the estimation of most, was her way. "I…I can't talk about it, Gabriel. There's nothing to say." And he had his own grief to deal with. So why bother him with hers? "It was a tragedy and I, um…"

"I understand," he said.

Gabriel's voice was so quiet it sent chills up her arms. Or maybe the chills came from realizing how much she wanted him to understand. But how could he, when she didn't even understand? She'd planned on going with Rosie, to be part of her sister's medical mission, but at the last minute Rosie had turned her away. Rosie, the dreamer whose plan had been to go to Peru and figure out what she was going to do once she was there, and Bella, the pragmatist who needed a plan set in cement before she'd budge. They'd argued about their different approaches that day at the airport, then she'd never seen her sister again. So how could Gabriel understand, when she didn't? "How's Ana Maria?" she asked, de-liberately changing the subject.

"Want to come see for yourself?"

"Are you sure?"

"I'm sure, Arabella." Slipping a gentle hand around her waist, he led her down the street. She was sure that, for Gabriel, it was an impersonal gesture, one that meant nothing. But for her it meant so much. And, for the first time since she couldn't remember when, a small ripple of calm washed over her. His benevolence, she decided. That's all it was. Gabriel was a benevolent man even in the midst of his own suffering. Something to admire, and she did. She was fooling herself if she thought it was anything more than that because it was only temporary, all this kindness directed toward her. At some point he would hear the whole story, discover the kind of person she truly was, and there would be no benevolence left for her. Not from Gabriel, not even from someone like Señora Escabar.

In the meantime, she was tired, her defenses were down, and she was enjoying her time with Gabriel. Later, when she was rested, she'd do better. She'd stay away, hide her heart again.

For right now, though, she'd savor the

strange, warm feelings seeping through her and be glad that, for the first time in weeks, she could feel anything.

CHAPTER FOUR

"I THINK she would have had her clinic closer to the landing strip," Father Carlos told Bella. She was sitting alone in the chapel, glad for the solitude. "We were hoping, of course, that she would come to Lado De la Montaña, but it's never wise to count on such things."

"Rosie always went where her heart took her. I think if she'd had a chance to know the people here, she would have stayed here."

"And you? Is that what you're considering?"

"I'm not like my sister. All she had to do was smile, and things happened around her. Good things, things people wanted to be part of. What I want doesn't always work out, and people aren't so drawn to me."

"Because you won't let them be?" Father Carlos sat down the pew right behind Bella, and leaned forward. "You're hard on yourself where you shouldn't be. People react differently to tragedies and it's not fair to think that we can all be the same, because we can't."

"You said her funeral mass, Father, and I wasn't there. On that day I was working, just like I did every other day of my life. There was no difference in that day and the next one or the one after that."

"But your work is a good thing. Helping people is always good, Bella."

But her helping was just another way to hide. "She was so devoted to setting up a clinic here. It's all she wanted, and I want to honor her in that. But I don't know if I can."

"When you find your heart, you'll find your way." He patted her on the shoulder, then stood. "So, what do you plan for your day? Because Señora Reyes is, as they say, great with child, and having a little struggle these past few days. I thought maybe you might go and see her, if you have time. I realise that you have yet to make a decision about working here, but I thought you might like to meet some of the people who could be your patients."

"I thought I'd go for a walk, but I'd be glad to see Señora Reyes first." As it turned out, Marisol Reyes was *very* great with child. A month away from delivering, Bella finally determined though the various language difficulties. Her blood pressure was a little high, not alarmingly so, and her ankles were swollen, again nothing to worry about. But she was tired, her back ached, and, from what Bella could determine, the baby was pretty big. Gestational diabetes was her first thought. The only problem was, there was no way to know for sure without doing a series of tests, and Marisol Reyes was going nowhere to get those tests.

"You have to watch your diet more closely," she told the woman, who merely nodded and smiled. "Do you understand me, Marisol? You have to be careful."

"I care," the expectant mother said.

Bella shook her head. "No. You have to be careful about what you eat." She said it in English then repeated it in her best broken Spanish. To which the woman responded by nodding, which told Bella that this conversation was in need of some serious help.

"Father Carlos said you might need some help," Gabriel said through the front screen door.

"I need a lot of help. I think I might have a case of gestational diabetes here, which I can't really diagnose. But I've been trying to explain some of the dietary consequences to Marisol, and I don't speak enough Spanish to get through to her. And she doesn't understand enough English to make a difference."

"Big baby?" Gabriel asked, stepping inside.

"Seems that way. Without an ultrasound…" She shook her head. "Let's just say that she's awfully big even for eight months along, and I don't have any reason to suspect twins. Couldn't hear a second heartbeat. And she's been eating sweets nonstop since I've been here. BP's a little elevated, ankles swollen—classic symptoms and no way to treat her other than keep an eye on her and work through complications that might arise."

"No coma más dulces, Marisol. Ellos no son buenos para su bebé. Coma alimentos frescos, las verduras, los alimentos que háran usted sano," Gabriel said to Marisol. Then to Bella, "I told her to quit eating sweets, that they're not good for the baby. To eat fresh foods and vegetables, and foods that are healthy."

Marisol put her hand on her belly, a slow frown crossing her face as the weight of Gabriel's words sank in.

"She understands," Bella said, then, through

Gabriel, told her to keep her feet elevated as much as she could. "She needs prenatal vitamins."

"No way to get them here," Gabriel said. "It takes so long traveling to a place where those kinds of things can be found that people don't do it very often. They don't even go after medical help unless it's critical."

Which was why Rosie had wanted to be here, Bella thought. "Maybe I'll go to Iquitos in a day or two and see what I can find for her," Bella commented. It was incredible what a lack of medical care meant in an area such as this, even in the little things. Rosie had talked about it, been passionate about helping in her own small way, but Bella had never truly understood. Until now. "Tell Marisol that she's to stay on bed rest as much as she can until she delivers, and that means no taking care of the house, no cooking for her husband. I'll talk to Father Carlos to see if there's some way we can get her some help. Also let her know that I'll stop by tomorrow to see her." Small measures. There were concerns ahead—keeping her blood pressure down without medication, the delivery itself, which could be difficult due to the baby's large size. So many things could go wrong, yet when she looked at the peacefulness on Marisol's face, the woman was not worried. She would do what she needed to do to take care of her baby, but what would happen to her when there was no doctor there to tell her what to do, or to help her with the delivery?

She could die, like Gabriel's sister had. The worry on his face as he looked away from Marisol told Bella that he was thinking the very same thing. Instinctively, she gave his arm a gentle squeeze. "Thank you for helping me with this," she said, her voice barely a whisper. "I know it can't be easy."

A deep sigh escaped him. "I, um…I need to get back to Ana Maria."

"And Marisol needs to rest." They both said their goodbyes to Marisol, with Gabriel giving a parting instruction to call either of them if she needed help, then they left the tiny cottage together, strolling casually along the road leading to Gabriel's house.

"Getting involved comes with strings, Bella. The more you help the people here, the more they'll depend on you."

"And that's a bad thing?"

"I don't know. Is it?"

"They're your people, Gabriel. You tell me."

"I suppose it depends on what you want to do with your life. If you really intend on opening that clinic here, you've just had your start. It's a good thing, if you really want to stay. But be very sure, because nothing here is like what you've ever been used to, and the way you'll practice medicine isn't anything you've ever done before. It's not going to be about popping into Iquitos to buy vitamins for one patient. I mean, that seems like a good thing to do, and in reality it is, but you're going to have to separate your priorities and, in the great scheme of things, ask yourself if using up an entire day is worth those vitamins, because that's pretty much what it'll take."

"You sound like you're trying to discourage me."

"Not discourage. Educate. Idealism is nice, but you've got to be practical."

Rosie had been idealistic. But she'd also been practical, and one didn't exclude the other. "Believe me, if there's one thing I'm good at, it's being practical." Her practicality had ended her engagement to a very nice man in San Francisco. Engaged for a year, she'd been too practical to marry him. So practical, in fact, that she'd sent James Cooper straight into the arms of a woman who'd wanted more than practicality from her relationship. "I have it down to a science."

"And you're not happy that way?" he asked.

"It's not a matter of being happy that way. It's just the way I am." The way she'd always been, the only way she knew how to be. The product of a heart without passion, James had told her the day he'd broken off their engagement. He'd accused her of not allowing herself to be passionate about anything, then he'd told her she deserved passion. Theirs had been an amicable parting, and they'd worked together for another year after that as medical partners. To be honest, it hadn't even been difficult maintaining the professional relationship after the personal one had died. To all appearances, there really had been no differences before, or after. "I'm reserved. You know, don't wear my emotions out there for everyone to see."

"But you don't smile. And your eyes are so sad most of the time. That's the first thing I noticed about you—your sad eyes."

"There have been difficult circumstances. And coming here hasn't been easy." They were at the entrance to the church now, and she stopped. "Just so you'll know, I am going to find a way to get those vitamins for Marisol. Maybe I can't afford to take a whole day to do it, but there's a way, Gabriel. I just have to figure out what it is."

He laughed. "I'll just bet you will."

"I'm going for that walk now," she told Father Carlos. "I had a look at Marisol, and told her she needed to do a little food adjustment. Put her on bed rest, too, so is there a way the ladies here can take care of her, at least as far as the cooking and household chores? I don't want her being any more physically active than she has to be."

"The ladies love being involved. Let me see what I can do to make arrangements."

It seemed so simple. Ask, and it was given. Too bad things weren't so simple back in her real life. But that life was filled with so many complications. Truth be told, today she'd gone out on her very first house call ever. Medicine didn't accommodate those personal aspects so much any more. Doctors didn't make house calls, for sure they didn't arrange home care from neighbors. If a patient needed to be seen by a doctor and couldn't come to the office, the solution was the emergency room. As far as home care went, that was arranged though the insurance company, which would hire a professional medical service to arrange any in-home kind of treatment or therapy necessary, and the paperwork was a mile long even to accomplish the smallest of tasks.

There was something to be said for walking a block to see a patient, then asking her friends for help. It worked. "I'll be back in a couple of hours," she told the priest, "and I'll stop back in to see how Marisol is doing. You wouldn't happen to know how I could get prenatal vitamins here, would you? Because I'd like Marisol to take them for the rest of her pregnancy if we can make the arrangements."

Father Carlos frowned. "That's one I'll have to think about. But I'll let you know what I find out."

Outside the church, Bella turned toward the road leading from Lado De la Montaña farther up the mountain. She didn't have a particular aim for this walk, except to get away for a while. She wasn't going out looking for the wreckage of her sister's plane crash since so many others had tried before, and failed. But she wanted to feel…connected. Connected to Rosie, connected to the others who had perished, connected to anything. And she couldn't feel that here. She couldn't feel anything here with so many people around, watching, trying to be kind. That's why she had to get away. The only thing was, no place seemed far enough. She could have walked forever and that wouldn't have been far enough.

"Could I send someone to escort you?" Father Carlos called, chasing after her. "If you've never been in a jungle before this…"

"I appreciate your concern, but I'd rather be alone for a while. And I won't wander off too far, I promise. Besides, it's already late, and I have a lunch appointment to keep." With the way the people of the village were taking care of her already, she'd have to be careful or she'd gain fifteen pounds in the next few days. It was like everybody here had taken her in, adopted her as one of theirs, and that went beyond the kind gesture of the meals they offered. They smiled at her, waved when she passed by.

It was a wonderful little village with warm, genuine people. Gabriel was lucky to have a home such as this. Did he even know how lucky he was? Because it seemed to her that he looked for a means not to like this village. It was as if his whole world revolved around what he had in

Chicago and Lado De la Montaña had turned into an afterthought. It was all a matter of what you wanted in your life, she decided. Obviously, Gabriel wanted the big, impersonal city, while she wanted…well, she wasn't sure. Not any more. In fact, it had become so much easier thinking in terms of what she didn't want that she wasn't sure she could even start of list of things she did want. "Look, Father, I appreciate your concern, but I'll be fine by myself for a little while. I just need time to think."

"You've suffered a terrible tragedy, my dear. You've lost a great many friends somewhere near here, and your sister as well, and it can't be easy to face so much sadness alone."

"You haven't told anyone about my sister, have you?"

A skeptical frown crossed the Father's face. "No. I don't divulge confidences, but I don't understand why you keep that to yourself. People would open their hearts to you even more than they already have if they knew. It's a tragedy to lose someone you love, Bella. I know the people here would want to help you through that."

"No, they wouldn't," she said stiffly. "Not if

they knew…" She bit off the words so close to spilling out. She didn't understand why that had happened after all these weeks of holding it all in, and attributed it to finally coming to Lado De la Montaña and being so close to where her sister… "Not if they knew that I didn't want to come here, not when it happened. That I refused all those times you contacted me. That…" That she had backed out of the trip with her sister at the last minute and accused Rosie of thinking with her heart and not her head where this medical mission was concerned. "That's something the people here wouldn't understand, because they want to be close, want to help each other. Outside what I do as a doctor, I don't, and they wouldn't like that once they saw it in me."

"I think you're reading some of your own confused emotions into other people, Bella. I'm sure your friends back home, as well as the people here, deserve much more credit than you're giving them. It's you who doesn't want to be touched by them, not they who don't want to be touched by you."

"You're right. I don't want to be touched, because in the end I ultimately hurt the people who get too close. So what I'm giving them instead of that personal interaction is honesty, for a change. As for confused emotions? There's nothing at all confused about my emotions. I'm hurt, and I'm angry as hell."

"Emotions that will mellow."

"Emotions I don't want to mellow. And, see…that's the thing. Everybody thinks they know what's best for me. *Give it some time, Bella. Think about the good times you had with your sister, Bella. Don't dwell on things you can't change, Bella*. It's all so…so lame. Words to fill in empty, uncomfortable spaces because no one can know, no one can understand." She stopped, totally shocked that she was unleashing this personal war with the village priest. He didn't deserve it. He was simply a compassionate man trying to show concern, and here she was, throwing it right back in his face. "Look, I'm sorry, Father. None of this is your fault and you don't deserve my anger. But it comes out at all the wrong times, which is another thing the people here don't deserve."

"You don't deserve it either, Bella. Neither do you deserve the guilt you've chosen for yourself."

But she did. Every last speck of it, and more. That's just the way it was, and it wasn't going to change. "If you see Cielo Alcantara, tell her I'll be back in time for the noon meal." She spun away, then impulsively spun back to face the priest, reaching out to squeeze his hand. "Thank you for trying," she said, her voice barely above a whisper. This time when she spun away, she didn't turn back.

"We're fine," Gloria Elena assured Gabriel. "Between the three of us, we'll take very good care of Ana Maria the rest of this morning." Two of his mother's friends had stopped in to see the baby and they were so busy fussing over her he doubted anyone would miss him at all. That's the way it had been since he'd returned home... friends dropping by to keep his mother company. People bringing gifts, food. He was grateful for the kind gestures as they kept her from dwelling on Lynda every waking moment of every day. So now, while the ladies fussed, he wasn't sure what he was going to do with himself. Maybe go and find Arabella.

Go and find Arabella—funny how that seemed the natural thing to do. "Damn," he muttered on his way through the creaky gate. He was establishing a dangerous habit with her. One that would come to nothing since she was leaning toward staying here, and he was definitely on the verge of going home…to his real home, Chicago. Too many differences, he decided as he flagged the priest down. Even so, he was still going to go find her.

"She didn't specifically say where she was going, but I think she's gone off to look for the airplane's crash site," Father Carlos told Gabriel. "On foot." He pointed toward the road to the west. "And I don't think she's going to be very happy if you go after her. Dr. Burke likes her solitude. In fact, she's rather emphatic about it."

"Maybe she's emphatic, but she shouldn't be alone out there." Gabriel glanced down the road, catching a glimpse of her just as she veered off onto a path he knew well. "People don't always know what's for their own good."

"Maybe so, maybe not. But there's a time for solitude, Juan Gabriel, and there's a time for friends. Keep that in mind because you may not get what you want when you catch up with her."

"Believe me, I do keep that in mind. All the time. But when it comes to solitude versus the company of friends, sometimes it's so easy to get lost in one that you don't recognize when it's time to surround yourself in the other. Look, if you're going by my mother's house, would you tell her I may not be back in time for lunch?"

"And if you have time this afternoon, do you think you could stop by and have a look at Alfonso Terrones? He's not been feeling too well lately—stomach problems, I think—and I can't convince him to go all the way to Iquitos. He says he's getting too old to travel that far any more. So I thought that since you're here, maybe you'd take a look. Or you and Bella could do it together, if you don't mind?"

Gabriel's attention was still focused down the road, where Bella had finally disappeared from his view. "This afternoon," he promised the priest, then took off in a run, kicking up dust from the road as his feet hit the ground. It was crazy, chasing after her this way, and he knew that. But what he knew didn't stop him. In fact, maybe it's what he knew that compelled him to pick up his pace when what he really should have done was turn and run in the other direction.

Father Carlos watched Gabriel until he was out of sight. Juan Gabriel had his own devils to deal with, Father Carlos decided. And a life ahead of him he wasn't sure Juan Gabriel was dealing with yet. "Maybe they'll find what they need in each other," he said to himself as he headed off to call on Gloria Elena. A smile crossed his face as he thought of the possibilities of the two doctors getting together. It wouldn't be the easiest course he'd ever seen, but the prospects held promise. Only problem was, neither of them would recognize it if it was staring them straight in the face. And it was. He was sure of that!

"I told Father Carlos that I don't need someone to go with me, and I meant it. So he sent you anyway?" she snapped. "Sent you to follow me, like I'm not capable of finding my way along this well-traveled path?"

"He didn't send me. In his own way, I think he tried to warn me off."

"And you didn't take the warning! Why am I not surprised?"

"I didn't take the warning because you're heading out into the jungle alone, which isn't the smartest thing to do even if it is on a well-traveled path. Ever heard of caimans and pumas and poison dart frogs? Not to mention jaguars?"

"I have a stick," she said, holding it up to show him. "Big stick."

"A stick and an attitude will still get you killed by a jaguar, Arabella. No matter how big that stick, or attitude, is."

A bitter laughed escaped her. "Haven't you heard? I'm the charmed one, the one who escapes death?"

"So why go looking for it in other ways?"

Bella stared up at Gabriel for a long moment, not sure how to respond to him. James had asked her once if she had a death wish. She hadn't eaten for days, hadn't taken much more than a sip of water every now and then. It hadn't been that she'd been trying to kill herself. She'd just lost track of time. No appetite together with interminably long hours of nothing and she'd gotten herself in a weak state without even noticing. But it hadn't been a death wish then, as it wasn't now. It was simply the vast numbness that surrounded her, sucking the very life out of everything. It had completely robbed her of all but breath and even at times wrestled her for that. "I don't go looking for it," she finally managed. "Believe it or not, I value my life. It's just that sometimes I…" What was she doing, standing out here confessing like this to Gabriel? First venting to the priest, now this? It had to stop! "Sometimes a walk in the jungle, *alone*, is just a walk, Gabriel. No hidden meanings or purposes, so don't go reading something into a simple walk that's really none of your business." She drew in a deep, steadying breath and squared her shoulders. "So now, please, leave me alone."

"I would, if I thought this is a simple walk, but once you find out that not too far off is a nice mountain stream where the villagers fish and the children swim, and what you're looking for isn't there, you're going to take another trail, one that's not so well traveled."

She didn't like the fact that he was right about her, as that's exactly what she *would* do. "You don't know that."

He laughed. "You're not as impenetrable as you think, Arabella. I don't mean to be insensitive, but you're here to look for the wreckage, and when you discover that it's not on the well-traveled path, you'll take the path less traveled, then one even less traveled than that. Even if you won't admit it to me."

"OK, I'll admit it. I'm looking for the…" The words hurt, even the ones she couldn't get out. But common sense had already told her the plane hadn't gone down anywhere in this direction. With such a well-used trail, it would have been discovered. So maybe that's why she'd chosen to go this direction her first time out—so she wouldn't find the one thing she dreaded most in the world.

"Looking in all the wrong places?" he asked, his voice so gentle it almost hurt. "Because that's what you're doing isn't it?"

She nodded reluctantly, rather than speaking, because she didn't trust her voice. So much could be given away in a little crack or wobble, and Arabella Burke was still clinging to the desperate hope that she had some control left. Although she was afraid that to Gabriel it was all transparent.

A man who knew her so well scared her.

"Look, Arabella, I can deal with you pushing people away, and I can even understand it because sometimes that's the easiest thing to do. But doing what you're doing right now, *alone…*"

"I, um…" Bella swallowed hard, willing her voice to stay steady long enough to see this through. "I'm perfectly capable of hiking in the jungle without someone tagging along to help me," she finally managed in a slow, deliberate cadence.

"That's just it. You're not. Not physically, not emotionally, and I think you know that, even though you won't admit it out loud."

"It's so easy for you to judge, isn't it?" The modicum of control in her voice she'd fought so hard to hang on to was gone and she didn't even care now. All she wanted—the *only* thing she wanted—was to be left alone, to have Gabriel and everybody else pretend they didn't even see her. She didn't want to be responsible to a meal list, or have the village priest worrying about her. She didn't want her friends back home speculating on whether or not she'd be fit to practice if and when she ever returned. No, she didn't want any of it. Yet it was all being forced on her under the gentle guise of something that was for her own good. "You've known me for a couple of days, and you think that gives you some sort of right in my life. Well, think again, Gabriel. There are no rights here, not when it concerns me. Do you understand? No rights, nothing. I came here to see the area, and when I've seen enough I'll return to the village. That's all there is to it, and I'm not looking for concern, pity, or anything else along the way."

"So it's fine for you to extend yourself when

someone else needs help, like you did to Ana Maria and me, but when you—"

Bella thrust out her hand to stop him. "*I said* I don't need help. The rest of it's irrelevant, and that's the difference between us. You did need help. So did Ana Maria. I do not."

Rather than being put off, Gabriel chuckled. "Are you always this stubborn?"

"What I am, Dr. Velascos, is none of your business."

He chuckled again. "I have this patient back in Chicago. Her name is Millicent Montrose, and although she won't tell me how old she is, I'm guessing she's somewhere between seventy and eighty. Feisty old woman. Smart. Always wants to be in control of the situation no matter what. And to be honest, I do respect that most of the time. Except for the time when I had to do a repair to her bleeding ulcer and she insisted that she was *not* going to have a general anesthetic during the operation, that she wanted to be awake for it. In fact, she told me she'd either be awake or she wouldn't have the surgery done at all, and I couldn't convince her otherwise. She told me she'd sue me if I put her under."

"What did you do?" Bella asked, in spite of not

wanting to seem interested in anything he was saying. But for the moment the doctor in her took over and she wanted to hear more about his problem patient.

"In the end, I had the anesthesiologist put her under general anesthesia. She was totally out because you can't do major abdominal surgery on a patient who's awake."

"But how did you convince her to let you do that?"

"I didn't. She convinced herself, once I had the surgical tech trot out all the knives and various instruments I'd be using on her. Including a tribal machete left to me by my father." He spread his hands in a wide gesture, separating them by a good two feet, grinning. "Big machete. Almost as big as your stick."

"You didn't?" she gasped, fighting back a smile.

"Sometimes you have to *help* people come to their senses. All it takes is a little friendly persuasion."

Finally, the corners of her lips turned in just the tiniest of smiles. "A *big* machete isn't friendly persuasion. It's a big bluff."

"OK, I'll grant you that point but, no matter

persuasion or bluff, it worked. So, remember when I said you remind me of her? In some situations, like Mrs. Montrose's, *or yours*, being subtle doesn't work."

"So what are you going to do? Drag out the machete and threaten me with it, like you did Mrs. Montrose?"

"Persuade," he said, keeping a straight face, although the twinkle in his eyes was unmistakable. "Not threaten. And, no, no machete or big stick. But I do want to be your friend, Arabella. It might not be quite as dramatic as what I did to Mrs. Montrose, but I think you do need a friend here, even if you're too stubborn to admit it."

Damn it, why did he melt her defenses like he did? She didn't want him to, and she fought hard against it, yet it happened anyway. She resisted him, then she gave in. More like totally collapsed. Poor Mrs. Montrose hadn't stood a chance.

She wasn't Mrs. Montrose, however. So, what was it they said? Forewarned was forearmed? *Well, this one's for you, Mrs. Montrose*, Bella said to herself as she turned away from Gabriel and walked on down the path. Alone. Without looking back. And definitely forearmed, even though she wasn't sure that's what she really wanted. Because, admittedly, having Gabriel walking by her side would have been nice. Except she didn't deserve nice any more. Which was why she walked alone everywhere she went these days.

Just this once, though, she didn't turn around and fight him off when she heard him follow her.

"My father used to bring me here when I was a boy. We'd spend the day fishing. Sometimes we'd stay into the night, build a fire and cook the fish right here."

It was a lovely area. A nice, lush canopy of trees overhead, shadowing the mountainside stream splashing its way over a bed of jagged rocks. It was surprising how the area was so well used, yet still nearly pristine, cared for by people who respected the abundance of nature they had here. So different from the city. And so quiet… She liked that, liked the peacefulness of it. "You were lucky," she said on a wistful sigh. "When I grew up, all I had was…city. Lots and lots of city." And no father to take her anywhere.

"Cities are nice. That's why I live in one now."

"This is what's nice, Gabriel. Cities are tolerable. They suit practical needs and take care of people who thrive on a hectic lifestyle. But this is what's truly pleasant. It suits the esthetic. And nurtures the soul. But I suppose it's easy to take for granted all the same, isn't it?"

"Why did you choose to volunteer with that group of doctors who wanted to start a mission hospital here, Arabella? Is that what suited *your* esthetic and nurtured your soul?"

"They needed a pediatrician, and I was about to become available." Available because she had been on the verge of quitting her practice with James. His wife had insisted that an old fiancée didn't have any place near a new marriage, and the situation had become increasingly uncomfortable. "You know the same old story. Involved with medical partner. He finds another woman, marries her and the little wife doesn't think having her husband's old lover working side by side with him every day is a good idea."

Gabriel chuckled. "Sounds complicated."

"Not really. We weren't suited personally. Professionally we were good, but once you step over the personal line the way we did and it doesn't work, it's hard to go back." That was the simplified version. Had she wanted to fill in the details she'd have told him that she had been the one who'd distanced herself from James, then kept pushing him away. She would have told him that James had loved her far more than she had been capable of loving him back. She would have told him that maybe she didn't even believe in falling in love, or that she couldn't, and she'd hurt a very decent man because of that. But she didn't because none of it mattered. She wouldn't do it again. "Why did you really follow me?" she asked, purposely changing the topic of conversation. "Even when you knew I wanted to be alone? You didn't really think the animals were a threat, did you?"

"Because you needed following, Arabella, and, to be honest, I don't know why. But I can see it in you, even if you refuse to see it in yourself."

"Don't take rights with me, Gabriel. And don't make assumptions. You'll only end up disappointed."

"I don't take rights. And I never make assumptions." He grinned. "Well, almost never. I suppose the machete was an assumption, wasn't it?"

"An assumption that you would get your way. Like you assumed when I said I didn't want you coming along with me that I really did? Was that how it was?"

"What I assumed was that you were coming to a place I very much wanted to visit." He shrugged. "I was right. You were."

"Well, I was here, and now I'm not. Don't follow me this time, Gabriel. I mean it!" Without another word, Bella turned and headed down a narrow path leading away from the stream, away from where she'd come. She wasn't even sure why she was doing that since she really did enjoy Gabriel's company, and she tried not thinking about it until she was far enough away from him she was convinced he really *wasn't* going to follow her this time. Then she sat down under a giant cecropia tree, its small, umbrella-shaped leaves giving her the shelter she needed, and pulled her knees up to her chest. On a dispirited sigh she dropped her head to her knees, shut her eyes and hoped, desperately, that the images floating around in her head stayed dark and distant.

This wasn't working. Coming to Peru wasn't helping her get past anything. If possible, she was more confused, more heartbroken than she had been before. The worst part was that she felt so…removed, not just from the good people here who truly wanted to befriend her but from herself. She was only going through the motions, and avoiding the emotions as she was doing so.

Then there was Gabriel. She was *so* drawn to him…attracted to him, amazed by him. Her natural inclination might have been to be a little clingy because a broad shoulder right about now, especially Gabriel's broad shoulder, would have been wonderful. That's why she was going out of her way to avoid him. She was off…so far off she wasn't sure she would ever be right again.

"I haven't been avoiding her," Gabriel argued, even though he knew his mother was correct. He had been avoiding Ana Maria. Ladies from the village flitted in and out all day, fawning over the baby, and there was always his mother, so why get himself so involved right now? Especially since he was about to have a lifetime of it ahead of him. Except, admittedly, there were moments when he found himself missing her, or thinking about her. He wasn't on the verge of fatherly thoughts or anything like that—planning her future, worrying about her first date with a young man he definitely wouldn't trust, dreading the day when she wanted to learn how to drive. No, those kinds of thoughts were pushed to the back of his mind, yet when he bent over Ana Maria's crib and looked down at all the innocence lying there looking up at him, trusting him, he couldn't help but wonder what kind of life they were going to have together. There were so many things he didn't know, things she would trust him *to* know. "I just went to see how Arabella was doing, then I took a walk down to the stream." Would Ana Maria want to go to the mountain stream with him, the way he'd always wanted to do with his father? Or would she prefer to go shopping in one of the fine Chicago establishments?

"Well, I'm going to go sit with Rocio Allavena this afternoon. She's not feeling well these days—arthritis problems—and I promised to help her stitch a quilt for her great- granddaughter. So you'll have to stay with Ana Maria."

"I have a patient to see." It was a lame excuse, but the only one he could come up with at a moment's notice. "I promised Father Carlos."

"I'm sure Ana Maria will do well with the fresh air when you take her with you." Gloria Elena stepped away from the crib, heading toward the bedroom door. "Look, Juan Gabriel, I know this isn't easy for you. But it wasn't easy for me, raising two children alone, after your father died. I had no money, there are no jobs here…you were old enough to see how difficult it was. But we managed. We always managed because we had each other. And, believe me, there were many, many nights when I cried myself to sleep, worrying about what would happen the next day…did I have enough food to feed you, could I afford new shoes for you, or school books? Ana Maria is lucky to have advantages you never had, and once you realize that just having each other is truly the only thing that matters, you'll be fine. It always worked for me, in those long hours at night when I worried so much. I had my two children, and that's what I thought about when I didn't think I could make it. You were my strength, Juan Gabriel. You and Lynda. Ana Maria will be your strength. You'll see."

Gabriel crossed the room and pulled his mother into his arms. "It's not easy," he whispered to her. "I want to be a good father to her, but I don't know how."

"No one ever said it would be easy. But you'll

be surprised what you can do when you have such a good reason for doing it."

Moments later, Gabriel stared out the front door at his mother, who was on her way to the cemetery beside the church. She went every day. He hadn't been there yet, despite the fact that he knew he would have to go there soon, amongst so many other things he had to do. He wasn't ready, though. Not for this, because going to the cemetery meant facing an unavoidable truth, and being slapped in the face with the knowledge that he was no longer in control of his life the way he'd wanted to be wasn't on the top of his list of things to do.

OK, he was avoiding it. He admitted that. Maybe it was an ugly side of him coming out that he just wasn't prepared to tamp down yet. Wasn't that his right? He'd been thrust into a situation he hadn't chosen after all! And, yes, he was angry. Not at anything or anyone. But he was angry that Lynda had died, and angry that Hector had abandoned his daughter and angry that…that he wasn't taking this change in his life better.

Maybe what made him angriest was the way he was acting. Damn it, anyway! This was a side of him he didn't like, one he hadn't expected. But life was made up of unexpected events. No one got to choose everything they wanted. And it wasn't even like he didn't want Ana Maria, because the truth was he did. The idea of being a father to her was growing on him. Scaring him to death, too. Most people had nine months to prepare for parenthood and he'd had about a minute. On top of that, he didn't have the good sense God gave a goose when it came to taking care of a baby. Sure, it was easy for Arabella. She was a natural. And that went without saying for his mother. But he was…inept. Inadequate. Ana Marie deserved better than what he had to offer her.

So he avoided offering. It was a bad solution and one he'd have to get over. Single men raised babies every day, didn't they? "And I'm not going to say it's woman's work, because it's not," he scolded himself aloud. "It's parents' work, whichever parent that might be." In this case, he was the parent. *The only parent.* And one beautiful little girl was depending on him no matter how huge his doubts about being everything she needed now, and for the rest of his life. Those doubts didn't matter a hang to her as long as she got her diaper changed when she needed it and her belly full when it was time. So maybe that's the way he needed to approach this whole parenting thing. One step at a time. Grow into fatherhood little by little, rather than taking the whole job on himself at one time.

He and Ana Maria learning together. He actually liked that idea—the two of them in this with each other. Somehow, that made it seem simpler. Better.

In the bedroom, Ana Maria started crying and he knew without even thinking that was the cry telling him she was hungry. Amazing how he was already distinguishing between her different cries. "Coming," he called, rushing to the kitchen to grab a bottle of formula. So many things were amazing, actually. Including his growing feelings for her. Amazing and frightening. Just like his growing feelings for Arabella. Only Arabella's needs wouldn't be tended to in the simple ways Ana Maria's were. "So tell me, little one," he said to the baby as he picked her up and carried her to the rocking chair, "what do you think I should do about Arabella? Since the two of us are in this together now, I'd appreciate your opinion. Should I leave her alone as she asks, or continue trying a little friendship on her, which is what I think she really wants? I mean, you like her, don't you? And I know I like her. But I'm not exactly thinking straight these days, so, since you're part of this whole situation now, what do you think I should do?"

Common sense screamed to leave her alone. In his real life, where all things looked totally different, he probably would have. But here, as he watched Ana Maria suck hungrily on the bottle, the only thing that truly mattered to her at the moment, it hit him that *this* was now his real life. Ready or not, it had started. And part of it was the growing feelings he had for Arabella. "Or maybe the more appropriate question is, what should I do about myself?"

In answer, Ana Maria burped, and spit up on his shirt. Yes, this was definitely his real life now. As real as it got.

CHAPTER FIVE

LUNCH TURNED INTO AN amazing affair, so much more than an occasion to eat a simple meal, because nothing about it was simple. And the Alcantara family turned out to be a fantastic Amerindian family—an indigenous mix of several native tribes and nationalities. Beautiful people, with their bronzed skin, black hair and wide, generous smiles. But what was more beautiful to Bella than just about anything else was the way they related to each other as a family. While Cielo Alcantara, her noontime hostess, assured Bella that the meal was not a special occasion, that nobody had put themselves out for her, she couldn't help but think that they were throwing a small, early-afternoon party in her honor, with the nearly two dozen family members there, crammed into the tiny living quarters, all offering her their wonderful hospitality.

In the group, she counted at least fifteen children, and half again as many adults of all ages, ranging from a white-haired couple, who seemed to be grandparents to most of the children and who spoke no English, to men and women who seemed closer to the age of Cielo, and her husband, Fernando. They spoke English in various forms and seemed proud of the accomplishment.

And the food…dear lord, how they fed her. Heaped bowls full of *arroz con pollo, sancochado, papa rellena*—chicken and rice, hearty beef stew made from yucca and sweet potatoes, stuffed yellow potatoes. Not to mention the plates piled high with fresh fruits, warm tortillas and the platters that attracted her most, the ones filled with sweets…*alfajores*, a lemon pastry, *turrones*, a fudgy nougat, and her new favorite, *lúcuma* ice cream.

Bella's first thought when she saw this feast was to be polite about it by taking a small taste of several dishes, but nearly an hour into the dining extravaganza she realized that she'd stuffed herself with well more than a bite of everything. In fact, she'd felt so good, so relaxed that she'd eaten so much she wasn't sure if she could even stand up, let alone waddle her way out the door and back to her room at the church. Afternoon nap, she decided. That was the only thing on her mind as one of the children led her to the only upholstered chair in the Alcantaras' home and indicated for her to sit down. Which she did, gladly, promising herself ten minutes and no more. Then she'd go home.

But the children piled around her feet once she was settled in and started playing games, all of them begging her to join them. Two of the girls had a little red ball and silver jacks...such an old-fashioned, simple little thing she hadn't thought of in years, and they were enjoying it with all the same glee that her pediatric patients back home showed when they played the video games she'd bought for the waiting room. Different toys, same glee, children were children and she was beginning to miss them, miss their laughter and optimism, miss their pure inno-cence. In her confused life her connection to the children was the only thing that saved her. That redeemed her.

"Ricardo usually plays with us, too, when he's feeling better," the little girl called Keylla said in Spanish. Keylla, who was probably about seven, had such a serious look on her face when she mentioned Ricardo's name that Bella felt compelled to ask her a question about the boy.

Every instinct in her body went on sudden alert, and she'd learned a long time ago to listen to her instincts. *"¿Está Ricardo hoy enfermo?"* Is Ricardo sick today?

The girl nodded, then rattled off in Spanish faster than Bella could understand, "He's like he gets sometimes after he's gone outside to play."

Bella looked to Cielo for clarification. As it turned out, of all the various adults present, she was Ricardo's mother. "Sometimes he runs too hard when he plays, then he gets tired and his breathing is difficult. We try not to let him play with the other children in the village too much, but he crawls out the bedroom window and we don't know it, there are so many people living here." She gestured to a veritable stairstep of children standing on the other side of the room, backed by the rest of the adults.

A clutter of people, and all of them living here. Bella could see how easy it would be to overlook a child. Or more than that, how a child could figure out a good way to sneak out when he wanted.

"Ricardo is my oldest, and I depend on him to

know better about the way he's supposed to play. But he's still a little boy who wants to do what the other boys are doing, and sometimes I'm so busy looking after the younger ones I just don't notice what he's doing the way I should."

One thing Bella had learned as a pediatrician was never, ever to underestimate the abilities of a child—especially a child with a goal. Children were the truest testament to the old saying about where there was a will, there was a way. It seemed Ricardo had both the will and he'd certainly found the way. "Tell me what he does when he's sick."

"His chest gets tight. And it's like his breathing is fighting against him."

"How long has he been like that?" Bella asked, making a mental diagnosis even before she'd seen the boy.

"Two, maybe three years. When it started it didn't happen so much, but now he gets sick more than he used to and it's so hard on him because he wants to be normal like the other boys in the village, and he can't. And they tease him."

"Has he been seen by a doctor? Is he on any medicine?" Before she finished asking the question, she could tell from the expression on Cielo's face that Ricardo, like most of the children here, had never been checked by a physician. It wasn't because the parents didn't care. They did. In fact, the families here were extraordinary. Loving, caring, protective... But there were so many extenuating circumstances that prevented then from doing the ordinary things, like taking their children for routine medical care—money, proximity to medical help, transportation. All the things Rosie had talked about. She'd told Bella that one trip to the doctor for a twenty-minute check-up could take an entire day and cost a week's worth of wages in gasoline and other expenses. That lack of convenience had been one of the driving forces behind her passion to practice medicine here.

"When we heard there was going to be a mission clinic built nearby, I thought I would take him to see one of those doctors. But after the plane crashed..." Cielo stopped abruptly. "Bella! I'm sorry! I'd forgotten they were your friends."

Just like that, it all came flooding back to her. It was never far away, even when it was cloaked in innocent statements like Cielo Alcantara's. "Do you mind if I take a look at Ricardo?" she asked, rather than dwelling on things she didn't want to think about.

"I had hoped that Juan Gabriel might look at Ricardo while he was here, but after Lynda died…" She paused for a moment, drawing in a deep breath. "I couldn't ask him right now. It wouldn't have been right with everything he and Gloria Elena are going through. But here you are, sent to our home like you were supposed to be here." Tears of joy streamed down her cheeks and she brushed them away. "Thank you, Bella," she said, sniffling. "Thank you. This means so much to me."

"After that amazing lunch you fixed for me, it's the least I could do." Besides, working was better than remembering, and it seemed that remembering, or trying not to remember, was all she'd done lately. Bella gave the woman a squeeze on the arm. "Now, could I ask one of the children to go to the church and have Father Carlos bring my medical bag here? It's under the bed, next to my suitcase."

"Teresa, you heard her," Cielo said to the oldest of the children huddled around. *"Corra rápidamente!"* Run fast.

Teresa was already out the door by the time

Bella headed down the hall to the bedroom. It was a narrow corridor, not much wider than her shoulders were broad, and dark, without a single light. The rooms she passed were all small, not tiny, but not overly spacious either, and there were several of these rooms, spaced one after the other on her left side. At least six of them so far. Bedrooms for all the families living together in this house, she supposed.

"He's back here," Cielo said, as Bella turned the hall corner and counted her seventh, then eighth bedroom. "In the last room at the end. It's where the older boys sleep."

The room was like all the rest, basic and filled only with beds and dressers for clothing, and little else. In it there were four sets of bunk beds all lined up against each other, literally spanning one entire side of the room, leaving barely enough space for a row of four wooden dressers backed up against the opposite wall.

Ricardo was huddled down in the lower bunk of the bed farthest from the door, so Bella climbed on her hands and knees all the way across the other three beds to get to him, only to discover there a child in the severest grips of an asthma attack. *Just as she'd expected.* "Is this the way he *always* has one of these attacks?" she called to his mother, who stood by the door, wringing her hands.

"Yes, but usually it's not so bad as it is today."

Untreated asthma scared Bella because it could be a killer in the way it methodically shut down the air passages. In Ricardo's case, he was in the throes of a severe bronchospasm, where his air passages were opening up to let the oxygen in then shutting off once it was, literally trapping it there so it couldn't be replenished with fresh oxygen. The sheer effort of forcing that air back out exhausted the body because it was starving for more oxygen, and the more it needed and didn't get, the more fatigued the body became. Without the means to diagnose Ricardo, Bella still guessed there was a marked increase in swelling in his air passages, trapping that air inside his lungs more and more each passing second.

The boy was wheezing hard, his respirations much too short and fast. He was also growing agitated because his brain demanded oxygen it wasn't getting in sufficient supply. At this stage, the brain started shutting down.

Laying her fingers to Ricardo's small wrist,

Bella counted a pulse of one hundred and thirty, which was well beyond normal. That, coupled with the way he was fighting so hard to breathe that he was using accessory muscles in his neck and shoulders, was a dire sign. "Ricardo," she said, readjusting her position so she could help him sit up. Lying down during an attack only made it worse. "I'm a doctor, and I'm here to help you." Not that there was much she could do without asthma drugs. "What I want you to do is sit up *and don't lie back down*. I'll help you. Do you understand?"

Ricardo's mother translated the instructions for him. Unfortunately, Ricardo was very sluggish to respond even to her voice, which meant his lack of oxygen was probably causing him some confusion now. "Listen to me, Ricardo. You have to sit up."

Ricardo did roll his eyes up at her, but rather than waiting for him to signal that he understood what he needed to do, Bella pulled him to a sitting position, held him in place, then propped a pillow behind his back. *"Más almohados, por favor."* More pillows please. Immediately six more were tossed at her.

Within seconds Bella had Ricardo sitting up,

nearly straight, against a wall of pillows. "Now, I want you to relax, and calm down." Good, encouraging words that sounded so calm when Cielo translated them, and sometimes staying calm was all it took to control an asthma attack. But not this time she feared after another minute without response from Ricardo. Not for a child who was scared to death the way Ricardo was.

"*¿Es médico usted?*" Are you a doctor? He choked out the weak words between breaths. Eyes shut, head slumped to the side, arms so weak that when she lifted one up then pulled her own hand away, it dropped like a rag doll's, Bella recognized that his stage of fatigue was advanced. Ricardo was fighting, but there was only so much fight in such a small body, and this was fast turning into a battle he wasn't winning.

Pulse one-forty and thready now. Lips turning blue. The rattling from Ricardo's lungs was so loud it could be heard on the other side of the room. In the best-case scenario he would have been hospitalized already, with the medicines he needed flowing into his veins and fresh oxygen from a mask going into his lungs. "How long do these attacks normally last before he gets over them?" she called to his mother.

"Sometimes they go away quickly. Sometimes they last a while. Maybe half an hour. Then he starts feeling better."

"*¿Ricardo, todavía me puede oír usted?*" Can you still hear me? Much to her relief, he tried to respond, turning his head slightly to face her. But the struggle for him to suck in a breath made even the simplest effort so difficult that he simply gave up trying and let his head sink back, limp, against the pillows. His eyes did flutter open briefly, though. And she understood the look she saw in them…fear. Pure fear. "*Defiendase,*" she whispered to him. "Fight back. I know it's not easy right now, but fight back, Ricardo. Think about every breath you take. Think about taking it in, think about letting it back out." Was he hearing her voice now? Was he hearing his mother's voice translate the words? With the way his eyes fluttered shut again, Bella doubted it.

"Your medical kit." Teresa squeezed into the tiny room and crawled her way across all the beds with it. "And Father Carlos has gone to find Juan Gabriel."

A medical kit that would do no earthly good because she needed drugs to end Ricardo's crisis, and she didn't travel with drugs of any kind any more. Most doctors didn't these days—it put them at too high a risk of being robbed. And the restrictions of air travel pretty well prohibited traveling with them if you did still carry anything with you. Bella doubted it would be any different with Gabriel, although she was glad he was on his way.

"Ricardo will be OK in a little while, won't he?" Cielo asked from the doorway. There was no confidence in her voice, however. Only fear.

"This is a severe attack. I don't know if it's worse than others he's had in the past, but he's having a pretty rough time of it right now." While Bella didn't need a better listen to his chest to know exactly what was going on inside, she positioned her stethoscope and listened to the wheezing anyway. It was bilateral, spread out over both his lungs, and the amount of air passing in and out now was so little she actually started going through a mental check list of how to proceed with cardio-pulmonary resuscitation should that become necessary. But to what end? That's what was scaring her, as she could perform all the essential lifesaving steps necessary, yet she had nothing to give him medical support to come after it. No oxygen, no medicine or IV fluids, no way to continuously measure his oxygen levels. Not even a good way to get him to the hospital because, as weak as he was now, Ricardo didn't stand a very good chance of surviving the long, bumpy trip off the mountain—not by truck or car, anyway.

"Arabella!" Gabriel called from the hallway, his footsteps pounding hard on the wooden floor as he ran to the bedroom. Father Carlos, who was a good foot shorter than Gabriel with half the stride, followed on Gabriel's heels, scrambling to keep up.

"Do you have any kind of a bronchodilator? Albuterol, or even a corticosteroid?" she called.

"No. Unfortunately, I don't have anything." Bending down, Gabriel began his crawl across the beds, tossing his medical bag in front of him. He stopped next to Bella, took one look at Ricardo, who was slumped so limply into the pillows now it was anybody's guess if he was still conscious. The expression on Gabriel's face as he instinctively took Ricardo's pulse told her he knew exactly how critical this situation was. And neither of them had what they needed to take care of it. Simple things. All they needed were simple things, and that's what was so frustrating. So little could have done so much for a dying little boy.

"He really will get better," Cielo called from her station by the door. "He always does, after he rests for a little while. He just needs his sleep now." The words of a mother whose hope was fading. "Sleep will make him better."

In a mother's estimation sleep might have been the cure, but in a doctor's view sleep wasn't Ricardo's friend now. "Is there any way to get him to a medical facility?" Bella asked Gabriel. "Helicopter?"

Gabriel shook his head. "Not easily. We can't get a helicopter in here, not anywhere close. No place to land. And you've traveled the road in… the *only* road in on this side of the mountain…so you know how bad that is. The one on the other side is better, easier to travel, but much longer, and either way it would take forever to get an ambulance here, if we could even get someone to send one, which I doubt anyone would. But maybe I could have an ambulance from the hospital in Iquitos meet us halfway."

"How long would that take?"

"At a moderate pace, maybe an hour and a half, if we're lucky."

"And at the pace we'd have to drive…" Much longer. Too long. Gabriel didn't have to answer her because the expression in his face told her everything she needed to know. In Ricardo's present condition he wouldn't survive the trip, no matter how short it was.

Meaning they were running out of options.

On a discouraging sigh, Gabriel wrapped a blood-pressure cuff around Ricardo's arm and took a reading. Then he listened to his chest. But rather than calling out results Bella already knew were bad, he simply shook his head.

"Have them meet us," she told him. "Find out how far they'll come and tell them we'll meet them there." It was a risk, but there wasn't another choice. The boy needed what they didn't have.

"I'll take care of that!" Father Carlos called. Outside the door, where he'd been standing, the crowd had grown to twenty people, all of them huddled together, none of them making a sound.

"Now, Gabriel, here's what I need you to do. I'm going to try something called progressive re-laxation technique…"

"Hypnosis?" He leveled a clearly puzzled stare on her, one that didn't doubt or decry her idea

but one that was more surprised than anything else.

"It can work, particularly in asthmatics whose
attacks *aren't* triggered by allergies. Ricardo's
are triggered by exercise, which is in our favor.
So I need you to speak for me since I don't speak
the language well enough. Much of the success
will be Ricardo understanding what you're
saying and connecting to your voice."

"Me? I've never done anything like this. I cut
them open to save their lives, but I don't talk
them through it in the way you want me to."

"I'll get you through it, Gabriel. You trust me,
Ricardo trusts you."

He nodded, reaching across and giving her
hand a squeeze. "I'm impressed. You have
hidden abilities I didn't expect."

"You know what they say about desperate
times calling for desperate measures." She was
glad to have Gabriel there with her, not only to
assist her medically but to give her confidence.
She'd never done this before. Practiced it, yes,
but had never applied it in a medical situation
or crisis. There was medical research to support
it, though. Research indicating a good outcome.
And all she wanted was that good outcome for

Ricardo, no matter how she went about getting it. But reading the research and applying it were two different things, and she was nervous because there really was nothing else to do, now. Quite plainly, it was this, or the boy would die.

"Well, I'd put my desperate times in your hands any day. In fact, I already have, with Ana Maria. And I would again."

"It's a controversial technique, and I wasn't allowed to use it in our clinic because it's not recognized as traditional medicine."

"Every little advance in medicine starts out as something that's not traditional. People resist it until it's proven valuable then suddenly it's traditional. If you think it's worth a try, I'm with you." Their eyes met briefly, then Gabriel gave her a confident nod. "And I trust you, Arabella, maybe even more than you trust yourself."

That meant everything to her. More than she'd expected it to. "Thank you," she whispered.

He smiled before he turned his full attention to the boy. "Can you hear me, Ricardo?" he said in words the boy could understand. "Dr. Bella did an amazing job helping my baby get better, and she's going to do the same thing for you now, too. But you've got to trust that this will make you better. Can you do that for me? "

His baby. He'd called Ana Maria *his baby*, but his voice had been stiff. Bella could hear it and for a moment she wondered if Gabriel and Ana Maria were bonding yet, or if he was still so detached from her, doing the right things for his little girl from an emotional distance. "Are you ready?"

"Ready."

He looked concerned, as he should have. But he didn't protest, didn't question her as she gave him instructions, told him exactly what to say, and when. "Good. Now, keep your voice low, quiet, and talk slowly. The way I'm doing now." She drew in a deep breath. This might be their *only* chance.

Gabriel nodded again, then began. "Ricardo, I know this is very difficult for you, but you need to concentrate only on one breath. Listen only to my voice, and take one breath. Take it in, take it in, take…it…in… Good. Now, let it out. Let… it…out. Good job. Now, let's do that again." He glanced over at Arabella, who smiled.

For the next few minutes Gabriel focused solely on coaching Ricardo through every one of his breaths, and while the boy struggled desperately with them, Bella did notice that after a little while he was actually fighting to match his breaths to Gabriel's calculated cadence. And Gabriel was concentrating so hard on this he'd shut out everything around him. What an amazing man, she thought as he continued to talk Ricardo through this breathing, breath by breath.

"Pulse one-thirty." Bella matched the tone of her voice to the dulcet tone of Gabriel's. To be honest, she was fairly hypnotized by it herself. Maybe even a little seduced. A voice for the bedroom, and silk sheets and candlelight. Which she didn't do, she had to remind herself. She had to shake her head to physically shake off the feeling coming over her.

"Ricardo," Gabriel continued, "keep your eyes closed, and begin to feel yourself relaxing. Relax, and breathe. Relax…and breathe. Relax…breathe. That's all you have to do."

"Pulse one-twenty," Bella whispered. "Blood pressure holding stable." She leaned over and whispered further instructions in his ear so not to break Ricardo's concentration, which seemed very good. All in all, she was encouraged by what she was seeing.

Gabriel smiled his understanding, then continued. "Very good, Ricardo. You're doing a good job. Now, think about your right arm. That's all I want you to think about. Your right arm. Relax your right arm, let it grow more and more comfortable. Let your muscles become loose and limp and even more relaxed until your arm feels so light it could almost float." Gabriel repeated that several times, then moved on to various other body parts…Ricardo's left arm, his legs, his neck, his shoulders, then finally his lungs. And amazingly, with each instruction, the vital signs Bella whispered back to him got better and better.

They were winning the battle for Ricardo. She felt certain of that as she listened to the boy's chest. His breathing was evening out, the flow of air smoother now, while the wheezes that had been so loud just minutes before were diminishing to where they'd become only audible through her stethoscope. After about twenty minutes of Gabriel's relaxation technique, she whispered more instructions to him, sighing in relief. It was over. Finally.

"Ricardo, listen to me. I'm going to count to five," Gabriel said, "and when you hear that number, your eyes will open and you'll feel relaxed and refreshed." He repeated his instruction then counted slowly to five, his voice a little less soothing and a little more awake and normal with each passing second. When he reached the magic number, Gabriel drew in a deep breath, braced himself, then said, "Eyes open, Ricardo! You're awake now, feeling better, breathing better."

Miraculously, the boy opened his eyes, and what Bella saw there wasn't the same fear she'd seen earlier. He was still frightened, of course, but not on the same profound level. What she saw in the boy's eyes was…trust. And the silent acknowledgment that all was well. As a doctor she felt gratified. But as a person she felt…connected.

"We did it!" Gabriel said, sounding totally amazed, looking totally stunned.

Without thinking, she threw her arms around his neck and hugged him. Naturally, when she realized what she was doing, and enjoying more than she had a right to, she tried pushing herself away, only to find that Gabriel was holding on to her.

"We're a hell of a team, Arabella Burke," he whispered in her ear.

She responded with goose bumps stampeding up and down her arms. Had he noticed the way she reacted to him? Dear God, she hoped not. She also hoped he hadn't noted the way she'd simply melted into his embrace when it had become obvious that it had turned into his embrace.

They were simply two people celebrating a happy moment. That's all it was, she told herself when they finally did break away from each other. But the goose bumps still running riot all over her said something altogether different.

The ride to meet the ambulance that would take Ricardo on to the hospital was a long, nerve-wracking one, taking half again as much time as it normally should have, with Gabriel driving painfully slowly to avoid the bumps and holes in the road. Cielo sat in the front seat with him, alternately praying, assuring her son that everything would be fine and thanking Bella and Gabriel for their help, while Bella stayed in the back seat with Ricardo, keeping a close watch on him. He was awake now, his breathing steady, but he was still a little weak. Nothing serious, though.

Fernando Alcantara, Cielo's husband, who followed along in the family truck, met up with them at the rendezvous point just as the medics anchored an IV in Ricardo's arm and strapped an oxygen mask to his face. It was more for the sake of precaution than anything else because Ricardo was already protesting the treatment. To be honest, he really didn't need to be hospitalized in his present condition but Bella wanted him checked in a regular medical setting, with some blood work and pulmonary function tests performed. More than that, she wanted the doctor there to give him an inhaler to be used when he felt an attack coming on. It was a short-term solution to a long-term problem, because she had no idea what the Alcantara family would do when that inhaler needed a refill. She was sure the public hospital would provide it at a cost they could afford, or even give it to them free, but what about the long trip to go for it?

That was the big question that couldn't be answered. In practical terms, the prognosis for that happening wasn't so bright when the trip to get it was nearly impossible for the Alcantaras, as well as for so many of the others in the mountain regions. It was a problem that worried her because there was no easy solution. It had worried Rosie, too, and Bella was beginning to understand why.

"That was amazing," Gabriel commented, once they were back on the road and the Alcantaras were safely on their way to Iquitos. "Hypnotism. Who would have thought it?"

"Actually, I don't like to call it hypnotism. That comes with a lot of negative, hocus-pocus connotations. You tell someone you want to hypnotize them and they automatically think you're going to have them do something crazy. You know, bark like a dog when the doorbell rings, cluck like a chicken when someone utters the magic cue word. Unfortunately, hypnotism has become associated with cheap parlor tricks."

"But you think it has a positive place in medicine?"

"You saw it for yourself. Actually, did it for yourself. And it works. So, yes, I think *progressive relaxation techniques* have an amazing place in medicine, in some cases. Ricardo's type of asthma, specifically, responds well to relaxation. Although I think under different circumstances it's easier and probably safer to treat with medication, and the result has a more predictable outcome. But when you don't have that available, then you try what we did and keep your fingers crossed."

"But you've never done it on a patient before?"

"Only a willing volunteer, who, like me, was learning the technique."

"So maybe you should write an article for a medical journal now that you've done it."

"Maybe *we* should write that article," she said, "since you were the one who actually did the work."

"Like I said, we're a hell of a team. Maybe we will write that article together." Gabriel chuckled. "Dr. Navarro told me you had a rare talent for treating children. He was impressed, Arabella, and so am I."

"Well, for a surgeon, you make a pretty good pediatrician yourself."

"Not me. Kids scare me."

"The way taking a scalpel and slicing somebody open scares me."

"But there's a certain logic to the body when you cut it open. You know what's supposed to be there and what's not supposed to be. If it's not working right, you know how to fix it—repair that bleeding ulcer, remove that tumor. It makes sense. But kids… When you hear that cough, or when they come in with an elevated temperature, there are so many things to figure out, and most of the time it's not logical. I mean, when I was still a medical student I had a toddler who came in into the emergency department. His parents didn't know what was wrong with him, except he'd been crying for hours. He chest was clear, eyes fine, no ear infection, no temperature. Stomach sounded normal, heart was ticking away. No reactions when I prodded anywhere. Couldn't find any bumps, bruises, cuts, sprains, broken bones. But there was a blueberry up his nose. A damned blueberry! It was dark, stuffed way back there so you wouldn't necessarily see it if you weren't specifically looking for something."

"Let me guess. That's when you decided you didn't like pediatrics."

"That's when I decided I didn't want pediatrics in any form. Blueberries up the nose are never logical."

She laughed. "Except in a toddler who has just eaten blueberries."

CHAPTER SIX

SHE was amazing. He couldn't remember a time when he'd ever felt this comfortable with another doctor. Or even with a woman, not that he wanted to think of Arabella in a womanly way. But it was happening. Right now, she was twisted, staring out at the scenery, and he was casting sideways glances, and not at anything that had to do with her being a doctor. He was acting like a randy schoolboy who didn't want to get caught peeking.

That embrace on Ricardo's bed…it had caused a whole lot of distracting thoughts rumbling around in him. The way she'd fit in his arms was so natural, the way she'd pressed herself into him, just for that instant, had been so arousing that had they not been huddled over a sick child, who knows what would have happened?

It was crazy. He was returning to Chicago in a few days, once he was sure his mother would be fine. Or once he'd convinced his mother to go with him. Either way, though, he was leaving, and even if Arabella hadn't made a conscious choice yet, it was becoming more and more obvious each time he looked at her that she was going to be staying. She was taking Lado De la Montaña to heart, fitting in there. Sure, she believed she was in the throes of making a decision, but knowing Arabella the way he was beginning to, he was sure that a subconscious decision to stay had already been made. Meaning they'd line in two different worlds. Had she returned to San Francisco, they could have worked on a relationship of some sort. Professional, personal. Both. Chicago and San Francisco weren't that far apart, and while he loved his practice in Chicago he could actually picture himself moving to San Francisco, if that's what happened down the line.

But she wasn't going home to San Francisco, and he had to remember that every time other thoughts about Bella crossed his mind. "So, have you given any more thought to starting a clinic up on the mountain somewhere?" Dumb question, since he didn't want to hear the answer. But from her mouth to his ears might put the silly notions out of his mind.

"I'm thinking about it, yes. No decision yet. Just considering my options."

"Wouldn't you miss…you know, a modern practice?"

"Honestly, I probably would. But sometimes it nice to be where you're needed, and there are hundreds of other pediatricians in San Francisco. The loss of one wouldn't even be noticed. But the addition of a doctor in a place where there's no medical care at all is a major life event for so many people."

Damn, she made sense. He wanted to look over at her, watch her reaction to her words, but he had to keep his eyes on the road now. It was too rutted to do otherwise. "I think your patients would miss you."

"The thing about not having a medical practice is you don't have patients. When I left, I left with nothing. James bought out my half, and that included my patients, by contractual agreement. So for me, whatever I do, it's going to be a clean slate. I start over, no matter where it is."

"Did you two work well together?"

"We worked in the same practice, but we never worked together, to be honest. James was a little more intense in his approach. He liked to wear a white coat and swing his stethoscope from his neck. I liked wearing jeans and T-shirts and anything that made my patients think of me as more of a friend. So, had the occasion arisen, I doubt we'd have worked well together at all."

For some curious reason he didn't understand, that made him feel better. The idea that some doctor back in San Francisco could have had the medical symbiosis they had didn't set right with him, as stupid as that was. He had no right to that jealousy, but that didn't change the fact that he was a little green-eyed, thinking about Arabella and James together professionally, or any other way. "But you were engaged to the man?"

Bella let out a heavy sigh. "Have you ever done something that seems right at the time, but a minute later you realize it's a mistake?"

"A minute?"

"Well, maybe not a minute, but let's just say that in theory we made sense, while in reality we didn't. So what about you? No marriages in your past, or engagements gone wrong?"

"I'm upwardly mobile," he said, realizing how utterly absurd it sounded. But it was the truth. He'd traded personal life for professional growth.

"Which means?"

"Which means the doctor doesn't allow himself much time to play."

"So, how's Ana Maria going to fit into all that? Being upwardly mobile doesn't sound particularly conducive to the duties of raising a newborn."

"Haven't figured it out yet. I've been offered the position as assistant department head, which is going to take even more of my time, so I suppose I'll have to do a better job of delegating."

"Babies need more than a little delegated time, Gabriel."

"And surgeons can't strap a baby to their back and go about their day like that's the normal thing to do. Of course, talking like this makes me seem like a cold-hearted bastard, doesn't it?" It was the truth, though. The only thing he knew was that he'd work it out some way. He just didn't know how.

"No. It makes you seem like a man with a big problem ahead of him. It's not going to be easy, and I'm sorry about that. But you're going to be good with Ana Maria. Once you figure out how the two of you are going to live your lives, you're going to discover that being upwardly mobile doesn't preclude having someone else on that journey with you."

"Well, I'm losing sleep. And it's not just because I have to get up two or three times a night to take care of her."

"Too bad you can't take everybody in Lado De la Montaña back to Chicago with you. They'd all love to help. That's what my sister loved so much about this whole area…the generosity of the people."

"Your sister?" Odd, she hadn't mentioned a sister before. Especially one who'd been to Lado De la Montaña. "I didn't know you had…" His words cut off as he slowed the car, then swerved to avoid a particularly deep rut. As he did so, the ground shifted back on him. Or it seemed that way because as he jerked the steering wheel one way, the car went in the opposite direction, coming to a jarring stop when the right front tire landed in the very rut he'd been trying to avoid. "Damn," he whispered, as he set the car in Reverse. But before he could put his foot on the gas pedal the earth shifted again, and the rut in which the car was stuck opened up even more. "Get out, Arabella!" he choked.

"What?"

He opened the driver's side door and fairly flew out, dragging her along with him. But before she was fully out of the car, the earth shifted again, pulling the whole front end of the rental car down into the earth even farther.

"Arabella!" Gabriel shouted, as he fell backward, and started to roll down the embankment along the side of the road. "Arabella…"

"Gabriel…"

Bella shoved on the car door, trying to force it open, but it was stuck. It did open a little, but not enough to let her climb out, and from her vantage point she could see that the other car door was stuck fast against part of what had been the road. Naturally, the windows wouldn't respond to the controls, wouldn't lower, and full-powered cars these days had no other way to roll the windows down. No handles.

Besides being stuck inside the car, unable to get out, the car alarm was sounding…an eerie, repetitive, staccato honk breaking loose from somewhere under the hood. Loud, even bleats split the air, mostly likely being heard by no one except the two of them. "Gabriel, can you hear me?" she shouted, rolling over on her back, hoping she had enough room and force to kick out the side window.

Nothing. Not a word from him, but he'd been OK when he'd climbed out of the car only moments ago, so she had to keep telling herself he was fine. Gabriel was fine. He had to be! And she was trapped…had to get out before another quake hit, turning the road into a sinkhole that would gobble up her car even more than it already had.

Sucking in a deep breath and holding it, Bella shut her eyes and kicked the car window as hard as she could with both her feet. Damn her rubber-soled athletic shoes, anyway. Not only did they *not* break the glass, they didn't even budge it, as in pop the whole glass sheet out, the way she'd hoped would happen. So she tried again, this time bracing herself even harder against the console and gearshifts between the two car seats. It hurt her back, dug hard into her kidneys, and didn't give her the best leverage, but there was no other way to go about this if she wanted to get out.

And she wanted to get out!

One more time, she thought, sucking in another deep breath before she gave the window a second good kick, this time giving in to the panic and frustration setting in. In doing so, she shrieked so loudly she got a good adrenalin rush going, which gave her the necessary strength to break that window. No more then five seconds later she was scrambling out, using the car door as her brace to push herself up to the road, which was about at mid-chest level, the hole was that deep.

It was only when she was lying flat on her belly in the middle of the road that she finally looked back at her little rental, discovering how badly it was being devoured by the earth. Its front end was more than five feet down, sitting at a forty-five degree angle with its nose crammed into the dirt wall of the hole and its back end barely jutting up above the hole where the road had been only moments earlier.

Seeing the dangerous situation as it was… that's when Bella started to shake. She'd read so many stories about how giant sinkholes opened up during earthquakes and swallowed houses and cars and people. "Don't think about it, Bella," she whispered as she pushed up to her knees and looked around for Gabriel.

She didn't see him anywhere. "Gabriel?" she yelled. "Can you hear me? Where are you?"

No answer.

"Gabriel!"

No answer again. He must have fallen over the edge. That thought caused panic to set in—hard, ominous panic reaching out its cold, bony fingers, threatening to strangle her. She had to find him. Had to help him. "Gabriel, answer me!" she screamed, her voice high-pitched from frustration and fear. "Please…"

Crawling to the edge of the road, she looked down. It wasn't a bad grade, thank God, more of a gentle slope but over some nasty, jagged rocks. The vegetation wasn't dense though, and she could see a good bit of the way down. Could see every-thing but Gabriel. But he had to be down there somewhere. He wouldn't have simply got out of the car and run away, leaving her there alone.

"Gabriel!" she shouted, hanging on to the edge of the embankment, her fingers digging into the dirt as the earth rolled underneath her. It was no worse than a ship hitting a bad wave but, still, Bella squeezed her eyes shut and buried her head in her arms, her face to the road, until the after-shock had played out. Then she looked down the embankment again, focusing on one sector after another, rather than taking a wide sweeping check. That's when she found him. After about two minutes of deep, focused scrutiny, she saw something that resembled a body.

A body! "Gabriel! I'm on my way." He wasn't too far away, his long body stretched out, face down, partially concealed by a bush. Not moving. Instinct, not common sense, took over and she scrambled down the embankment, giving no thought to how steep it really was. Tripping her way down the dirt and loose rocks, she took a tumble herself, landing on her backside, then righted herself and continued, taking another tumble, this time leaving half the skin on her elbows in the dirt. But she got to Gabriel and dropped to her knees beside him, immediately feeling for a pulse. Strong, thank God. But what about other injuries?

"Can you hear me?" she asked, starting an immediate assessment, without turning him over on his back for fear he might have a spinal injury.

Running her fingers lightly over the back and side of his head, she felt a sticky trickle she assumed to be blood over his brow, but she didn't dare turn his head enough to have a look. "Wake up, Gabriel. It's a whole lot easier examining a patient for injuries if the patient can tell you where to look." Silly thing to say, but she had to talk, had to stay connected to him. "And I need you to navigate me back to the village. My car…" She choked off her words as he moaned. Good sign. It meant he was coming to.

"Don't move," she warned him, when he moaned a second time. Fat lot of good it did, though. Because on his third moan he tried to roll over. But Bella had anticipated that, and thrown herself almost entirely over his body in an attempt to stop him. "Stop it, Gabriel," she yelled at him, hoping her voice would break through his fog. "I haven't examined you yet. I don't know…"

He moaned again, and this time rolled all the way over, effectively throwing her off him and landing her flat on her bum. "I'm not dead," he said, sounding a little surprised as his eyes fluttered open.

"No, you're not dead. And you're not a co-operative patient either." She scrambled to her knees then crawled back over to him, already feeling the bruise on her rear end. "Now, listen to me, Gabriel. You were unconscious for a few minutes, I think you've been injured, but I haven't checked you yet. So don't move. Do you understand? Don't move until I've had a look at you."

"I'm fine," he grunted, moving his feet in circles in spite of her warning.

"You're a bad patient. Stop it, Gabriel!"

"No spinal injury," he said, as he lifted his arms, then winced. "But one broken or dislocated shoulder, I think."

"*I said* don't move."

He shook his head, like her words were finally sinking in. "I think I was dazed."

"Or stubborn," she muttered, positioning herself to examine his arm.

"You're cute when you're angry, Arabella. I see a nice glow under all that dirt on your face."

"That's not anger, Gabriel. I was scared." Angry, too, but he didn't need to know that. A gentle probe of his upper arm elicited quite a wince from him. "When I got out of the car and couldn't find you…"

"You thought I'd gone off and left you?"

"I thought you'd fallen off the mountain." She moved her exam higher on his arm.

"Damn, that hurts like a like a son of a…" He bit his bottom lip against the pain as she probed, then when she eased off raised his right hand to her cheek, brushing his thumb gently across a contusion there. "You're bleeding. Are you OK, Arabella? You're not hurt, are you?"

"Just a few cuts and scrapes. Nothing serious." One cut above her eye, and another on her cheek. Her elbows and knees were scraped too, and there were probably more battered places she hadn't yet felt. But right now all she noticed was the gentle way his thumb traced down her cheek, across her jaw…so light against her skin. Mesmerizing. It felt so good she wanted to linger there for a moment.

But as if nature were conspiring to remind her where she was, the ground shook underneath her in another aftershock, effectively breaking the magic of Gabriel's spell. Bella sucked in a sharp, ragged breath—one that had more to do with the quake Gabriel had caused in her than the earthquake. Such a sensual touch, and so reassuring, yet here he was, the patient comforting the doctor, while she was the doctor who should have been comforting him. "But overall I'm fine," she managed. "Lucky, too, I guess."

"We both are," he agreed, finally breaking the connection between them when he pulled his hand away. "But now I think it's time to assess…" Suddenly, the full force of where they were and what was happening came crashing back in on them in the frightening sound of the low, jet-engine-like rumbling that emanated as a forerunner to much worse things. It snatched their attention, an awareness of what was about to happen again and, immediately Bella pitched herself forward on top of Gabriel, who wrapped his right arm around her and held her as tightly as he could while the earth literally rolled and bucked beneath them.

Like an airplane crashing to earth, Bella thought, all the horrible images and memories flooding back to her. They grabbed hold, trying to seize her by the heart and squeeze the very life out of it. She couldn't stay there. Couldn't breathe. Couldn't think.

Had to get away. Had to run. Hide. "Let go of me," she screamed, trying to force herself away from Gabriel even though the earth was still shaking. But he only held on tighter.

"Leave me alone!" Bella struggled against him as dirt and rocks from the embankment above them pelted down like a convulsive storm, hitting and stinging them, bruising and cutting their exposed areas of skin. "Gabriel, please…" She thrust herself away from him, pushing off him with her foot, kicking his side, much the way she'd pushed out the window in the car, effectively breaking his hold on her. Then she tried to roll away, but he rolled over and caught her arm, grunting and straining from the pain. And he wouldn't let go as she fought him, harder now, hit at him with her fists, tried kicking him. "Let go of me," she screamed over and over. "Please, let go of me!"

"Arabella!" he yelled. "Stop it! Do you hear me? Stop it!"

"I can't," she cried. "I can't stay here. I have to…"

In one swift burst of energy, Gabriel yanked her back down on top of him, and nearly collapsed in doing so, fighting to hang on to the thinnest thread of consciousness left in him as the pain split through him. "Please, Arabella," he gasped. "I can't…" His world was wavering in and out now, almost as much as the earth was still wavering underneath them. "I can't hold on to you." Prophetic words as his arm had already dropped away from her before they were spoken.

Immediately, Bella bolted away, intent on running, but when she pushed herself up to her knees she noticed the way he was breathing so hard, the way he was wincing in pain, the way his eyes were squeezed shut. His face was scarlet, he was diaphoretic… Then suddenly the panic drained out of her in one swift purge, and the doctor inside took over. She couldn't run away from him. He needed help. There wasn't another thought in her but to take care of Gabriel. "Gabriel," she said, crawling back to his side. "Tell me where it hurts." Thank God the quake had diminished to aftershocks again.

"Shoulder," he forced out. "Head, too, but mostly shoulder."

She laid her fingers to his pulse, did a quick count, although her wristwatch was shattered. Even without an accurate measure she could tell it was too fast. Too fast, but strong, like he was. That was good. It meant there was a pronounced possibility he wasn't bleeding internally or else he would have been shocky and his pulse weak. That wasn't the case, though. "Let me have a look…"

He shook his head and drew in a sharp breath. Cold, pain-laden sweat dripped off his forehead and dribbled into the dirt underneath him. "You need to get back to the village…Ana Maria, my mother…everybody. They'll need help, and it'll take me too long to get back there. You go ahead. I'll come along later…slower pace."

Slower pace? Not a chance. He intended to stay right where he was and if something happened to her, and she couldn't get back here later on to help him… Unthinkable. She wasn't leaving him there alone. "No. I have to stay here with you," she said, moving her hands to his left shoulder to do the assessment. As best she could, given the circumstances, she checked Gabriel for motor, sensory and circulatory problems, relieved to find that only his motor function, or movement, seemed impaired. The joint was warm to the touch, and sensitive to the touch as well, which was a good sign as that meant the likelihood of bleeding going on in his shoulder, specifically deep in the bone, was slim. And there was no swelling, which was another good thing.

"Look, Gabriel, this is going to hurt. You know that." Her fingers probed deep to the bone while he gritted his teeth and held his breath, and she could almost feel sympathetic pain for him. This was excruciating, especially without pain medicine. But if he was lucky… Shutting her eyes, effectively shutting out everything but the feel of Gabriel's shoulder, she concentrated on the contours of the bone, visualizing in her mind what she was feeling.

"I think you're lucky," she finally said, after about a minute.

"Lucky?" Gabriel let out a string of expletives, then apologized, and let out another string of expletives as she continued to probe. "How the hell can you call this lucky?"

"Lucky because it's a dislocation, not a break, as best I can tell. And I'm pretty sure I can do a reduction and get it seated back in its socket." Meaning, literally, to reduce the injury or, in this case, pop the shoulder back into place. When a dislocation was fresh, it was usually a relatively successful means to make the patient more comfortable. Being stranded out here as they were, a reduction would also help Gabriel get himself back up on his feet so they could try and return to the village. *Together.*

"Just dandy!" he snapped, biting down on his lower lip. "Full dislocation?"

"No. A partial. *Subluxation.*" Meaning the head of the upper arm bone, or humerus, was partially out of the socket, or glenoid. "You've got some anterior instability—" it had slipped forward "—but that's easy to fix. Which is why I'm going to use the Spaso technique."

"The Spaso technique? Why would you be current on reduction techniques? You're not an orthopedist."

"In a pediatrics practice you have to be a little bit of everything. Sometimes that's an orthopedist. So what we're going to do is get you in a nice, comfy supine position…"

"Comfy?" he snapped. "Why don't you just leave me the hell here for now? I'll be fine until someone can come after me."

"I don't leave *anyone* behind," she said, unbuttoning her shirt then pulling it off to give herself more mobility. "I left someone I loved very much out here in this very jungle once, Gabriel, and I'm not going to do it again. Besides, a dislocation hurts a whole lot worse than it is serious. Once I get it popped back into place, you'll be almost as good as new."

"And the cure is worse than the injury. You know that!"

"But only for a little while."

"Are you going to hypnotize me?" he grumbled.

"Do you want me to? Because I could, except I don't think you'd be the most co-operative patient right now." Laughing, she straddled him, then looked down, studying his physique for a moment. Nice physique. Good muscles, broad chest. The assessment wasn't purely from a doctor's point of view either.

"What I *want* is for you to go back to the village, see who needs help, check on…my baby."

His baby. He'd called Ana Maria his baby, again, which meant it was growing on him now. Gabriel was undergoing a change of heart, even if he didn't realize it. But she did. She realized all the nuances, and that made her happy for the both of them. "We'll get there together, in just a little while. After I do this…" Bending, she grasped Gabriel's affected arm by the wrist, then lifted it vertically. Very gently. "Sorry I don't have a pain pill for you," she said, when he winced.

"Whiskey would work," he muttered through his teeth. "Lots of whiskey."

"Then I'd have to carry you back, and that would slow me down." When his arm was fully vertical, she pulled up even more, applying pressure as she pulled, and at the same time rotating the shoulder externally.

Reacting instinctively to combat the pain,

Gabriel raised his shoulder in the direction she was pulling it. So she stopped for a moment until he adjusted to the pain level, and once he had she continued to pull. Traction, essentially. She was acting as the traction machine, moving his shoulder joint back into place by degrees.

Twice more, Gabriel adjusted to the pain and she was forced to stop for a moment. Unfortunately, the humerus didn't seem to be slipping back into the socket as easily as she'd have liked so, while maintaining the upward pull to his arm, she bent even lower and gently pushed on his shoulder. Then suddenly she felt the pop she'd waited for. The reduction was complete and his shoulder joint was back in place. Just like that his pain level went from excruciating to dull ache.

Would his shoulder stay in place? That was another issue altogether. Sometimes that happened, sometimes the joint popped back out, possibly requiring surgical repair. For now all they could do was hope for the best, and make sure he favored it. Maybe get an X-ray when he could.

On impulse, Bella fashioned a sling from her shirt to tie around his neck. It would hold his arm and, in essence, keep weight off his damaged shoulder.

"You still conscious?" she asked, shifting her attention to his face. He was a bit pale now, and his breathing a little labored, but overall he looked none the worse for what she'd just put him through.

"Barely."

She laughed. "I think you're good to sit up."

"It would be easier if you hadn't kicked me in my ribs," he grunted without so much as a flinch in the direction of getting up.

She had. And she felt terrible, now that she remembered it. "How about I help you get up to the road right now, then I'll apologize later?"

"You're damn right you will. Apologize, and explain. *Everything*."

She glanced down at him, their eyes locking briefly. What she'd expected to see there was residual pain mixed with anger, but the only thing in his eyes was concern. For her. "I think I probably bruised you," she said, bending down to help him first to a sitting position, then tying the sling around his neck. For an instant their faces were so close she could feel his breath on her cheek and in that instant awareness surged through her body, her soul. But it scared her, especially for all the things she was, and mostly for the things she wasn't. "Bad arm in the sling, good arm around my neck," she said, "and on the count of three…"

"Why are you so afraid of me, Arabella?" he asked.

"It's not you I'm afraid of. It's…" She shook her head. "On the count of three, we're going to get you up. One…two… three…" With relatively little effort she helped Gabriel to his feet then, to avoid questions or eye contact or more awareness, she turned her attention to the embankment. How were they going to get to the top? It wasn't steep, but for Gabriel it was going to be a challenge. "I don't think there's going to be an easy way to do this, and I'm not even sure I can be of much help."

"There can be an easy way," he responded. "If you go on, and let me do this at my own pace. I'll be fine, Arabella. You don't have to worry about me."

"The only thing I'm worried about is the embankment, Gabriel. That's all there is right now. One embankment to climb."

"Like life. One embankment at a time. That's all we have to overcome, isn't it?"

In her life there were so many embankments.

"Look, I'm not sure how to do this. Maybe you should go first, and I can stay behind you, kind of pushing when you need it. Breaking your fall if you slip."

"Breaking my fall?" He shook his head. "You go up first, and let me deal with the embankment the best I can. Worry about *yourself* first, Arabella. For once, worry about *yourself*. And if I can't get up, this time you *have* to go on without me. They're going to need medical help in the village, and there's no other choice."

She swallowed hard. "I know," she whispered.

"But it's not like you're leaving me here," he said, pulling her with his good arm against his sore ribs rather gingerly. "Just think of it as my staying here to commune with nature for a while. Maybe that will make it better for you, because I *will* get there. I promise."

She rested her head lightly against his shoulder, trying not to hurt him any further. But only for a moment. Then she pulled away. "No risks, Gabriel. Whatever you do, no risks. Promise me."

"I promise. But life is a risk, Arabella. No matter how you take it, there will always be risks."

"That's the problem, isn't it? When you so desperately need the safe, level ground, it's not there to be found." Impulsively, she raised herself on tiptoe and kissed him on the lips. It was brief, tender, and as much a surprise to her as it was to him. But it felt right and in a life where nothing had felt right in such a long time, something finally made sense. "I'll see you at the top."

Getting to the top took Bella only about five minutes, but it took Gabriel nearly fifteen as they were impeded by a series of aftershocks, one after the other. None of them bad, thank heavens. But finally he did make it to the road, where he stood next to Bella for a moment, sliding his arm around her waist as they looked at the car sitting precariously in the sinkhole. "My medical bag's in there," he said.

"Mine, too. Which means..." She inched her way toward the hole, then looked down. They weren't going to be of much use without the few instruments they had somewhere down in that sinkhole, and there was no way of getting around that. "I'll be back in a few minutes."

Bracing herself for the climb back down, Bella dropped to the edge of the sinkhole, carefully pushing herself over the edge of it and straight through the broken car window. As she did so, the car shifted, the front end plunging down a good two feet more as the dirt underneath it gave way. *If I get out of this one alive…*she vowed silently, then didn't finish that thought as she crept over the front seat and found her own medical bag on the floor behind the driver's seat. Had Rosie thought the same thing—*if I get out of this one alive*—when the plane was going down? Had she thought anything else?

It's funny, how she'd never considered Rosie's last minutes. Only her demise. Yet her sister's last minutes seemed so…so close, so real all of a sudden, she could almost feel them. More real than she'd ever wanted them to be.

"Found anything?" Gabriel yelled down to her, jolting her out of her bitter-sweet thoughts.

"Mine." She looked around for a moment, and found his medical bag wedged between the far door and the seat. It took her a short time to yank it free, and when she did, the car rocked again, but this time it rocked because the earth was moving. Another earthquake! Or aftershock! She had to get out now. Get back to the surface before…

The plain, bitter taste of fear burned her throat as she scrambled back to the front window.

That's when she noticed… Dear God! The hole had opened up even more and she was not only shifting, she was sinking. All these past weeks and she would have welcomed her fate in a sinkhole but now…now she wanted to get out, wanted to get back to Gabriel. She wanted to live! "Gabriel!" she shouted. "I'm going to throw the bags to you." And hope she had enough time to get out of there herself.

The first bag went up relatively easily. The second hit the edge of the hole and bounced right back to her, forcing her to lunge after it before it fell somewhere beneath the car. But as she lunged, the car teetered even more and a large chunk of the dirt wall holding it in place gave way, sliding downward and burying the front end completely. Even as the car was being buried, it was still shifting under the rolling wave of the ongoing earthquake. She had the bag in her hand, though, and gave it one hard toss, hoping it landed right because if it didn't, there was no time left to readjust. She had to get out. Time had run out.

"Got it!" Gabriel shouted. "Now, get the hell out of there, Arabella."

It wasn't like he had to tell her to do that. The

second the medical bag left her hand, she climbed on to the top of the car, spitting out dirt chunks, trying not to breathe in any more dirt than she had to. It was dark, and she was far down now. There were at least seven or eight feet above her head to the surface, but, thank God, she wasn't sinking any more. That had stopped, leaving only the shifting dirt to threaten her. But her only option was up. How could she do it? How could she crawl up there?

"Gabriel," she choked out, batting away the falling dirt.

"Arabella, look up!"

She did, but all she could see was more dirt... and rocks. "Where? What?"

"Look up, Arabella. Keep looking up. It's there."

Eight feet to the surface...so close, and so far away. But she saw it. Her shirt...the one she'd used as a sling. It was twisted into a rope of sorts, tied onto his shirt, and dangling over the edge of the hole.

Reaching up, Bella grabbed hold and began to pull herself up...up...fighting against the dirt still sliding down on her, struggling to find footing against an earthen wall that was giving way, and walk up the wall as she pulled herself.

It was only a few feet, but it felt like a hundred, fighting against the cascade of dirt trying to push her back down. Gritting her teeth, Bella forced herself not to think about the burning, shooting pain in her muscles now, or the dirt in her eyes, nose, mouth that threatened to asphyxiate her. She was so near, but so close to giving in…

"Arabella!"

The hand came from nowhere to grab her wrist, and that's all it took to give her that last burst of energy she needed. Then she was on the ground, breathing fresh air, coughing dirt from her lungs. "Gabriel," she gasped. But he didn't respond. Instead, he scooped her up into his arms and carried her to the side of the road, well away from the sinkhole that had caved in completely on itself now and was threatening to open up even wider.

"Your shoulder," she managed to get out.

"Dislocated," he said. "I think you'll have to fix me again."

"Let me catch my breath for a minute first." Bella shut her eyes, expecting a vision of Rosie's face to haunt her, the way it so often did. But the face there was Gabriel's. Only Gabriel.

* * *

The walk to the village took nearly an hour, with both Gabriel and Bella practically holding each other up along the way. Several aftershocks hit them en route, and debris that had fallen down in the road threatened to block them in several places. But beaten down, injured, dirty and exhausted as they were, they finally made their way back to the village to discover that a number of the houses there had been damaged or destroyed, as they'd expected. Once Gabriel saw that his mother's home had sustained severe damage to the front, he left Bella standing in the middle of the road, trying to figure out where to start her assessments first, and ran straight to the house, only to find that no one inside answered when he called.

Frantic to know if his mother and Ana Maria were still in there, he tried to pull away tumbled boards and roofing from the front, ripping at them with his bare hands without regard to his injuries and making very little progress at getting through. So he finally gave up and ran to the rear of the structure, only to discover just as much damage back there. *"¿Gloria Elena, dónde está usted? Está usted ahí adentro?"* Where are you? Are you here? He shouted frantically, his voice breaking over the cries of children up and down the street and the shouts of other frantic people looking for other survivors. Where was his mother? And Ana Maria…the child he hadn't wanted, and the child he'd decided grudgingly to raise only because no one else wanted her. Where was she? He had to find her. To protect her. Keep her safe. Because he was her…father. He was Ana Maria's father. She was his…his daughter. Dear God, his child. She *was* his child. "Ana Maria!" he shouted frantically, pulling away debris from the back of the house, hoping the way in from there would be easier. But the more he pulled the boards loose, the more the house fell in.

"Vincent!" His mother's neighbor was standing in the yard, surveying his own wreckage, too stunned to make much sense of it. "Can you help me? I need to find my mother…and my daughter."

Vincent looked across the lawn at Gabriel, but there was no recognition on his face. Nothing but numbness. The same numbness he saw in Alfonso Calabrese, the neighbor on the other side, who sat in a lawn chair and simply stared out at the road rather than at the collapsed heap of rubbish that had been his home. Gabriel's heart hurt for these people. He wanted to help them on their own searches, but he couldn't. Not until he found his family.

For the next ten minutes Gabriel methodically pulled away board after board, as the pain in his shoulder threatened to rip him in two. Every joint, every muscle, every tendon in his body burned, but he had to get through. Had to find them. No matter what the outcome, he had to find them.

Twisting and tearing debris away from the pile, that's when it hit him. *Arabella.* She'd lost her friends, people she would have worked with here, and she hadn't had closure. That's why she was here now. He was sure of it. Sure that's why she wasn't healing. The incision that had cut her life in half was still open, and now that he couldn't find his mother and baby, he knew how utterly devastating that felt. Dear God, the pain of not knowing! He understood. He truly understood. "Ana Maria!" he shouted. "Mamá!"

"They're in the church," Bella called, running up behind Gabriel. "Safe. Both of them. Father Carlos is taking in the people who lost their homes, and your mother and Ana Maria are there, among them."

Frantic and focused, he kept ripping away the boards, not hearing her.

"Gabriel, stop. Listen to me. They're safe. Your mother and daughter are safe." She stepped up behind him and grabbed hold of his arm to physically restrain them. "They're in the church. They're not hurt."

He dropped the board he'd pulled from the pile and let it fall to his feet. "You're sure it's them? You saw them yourself?"

She nodded. "I talked to them. Ana Maria's a little cranky, but so are all the babies there. And Father Carlos says he believes he has every baby in the village safe in the church now. I need you to go stitch him up, maybe tie him down, because I'm afraid he's going to pass out. Then I need to have a look at all the babies to make sure…then the children, and…" Her words were tumbling out so fast they were difficult to understand.

"Stitch who?" Gabriel asked, effectively slowing her down.

"Father Carlos. He has a nasty cut on his head, and he's lost too much blood. I'm worried about him because he won't slow down, and he does need to get off his feet for a while."

"Slow down yourself, Arabella. You're as bad as Father Carlos."

Bella drew in a deep, steadying breath, then slowly let it out. "There's so much to do. It's making me frantic."

"Which is why we need a plan. You know, figure out where to put the people who are injured, decide how we want to go about a house-to-house search for survivors, find a way to get medical supplies into the village."

"You're always steady like this, aren't you? No matter what, you're always steady." She looked up at Gabriel for a moment, then tumbled straight into his arms. Arms that were ready for her. And there, in the middle of the road, they stood clinging to each other for a little while, but not as long as either would have liked. Duty called, and they were the only ones there to answer it. Finally, when they knew they'd spent all the time together they could, Gabriel tilted Bella's face toward his. "You're a filthy mess, you know."

"I know," she whispered.

"Blood and dirt caked on your face."

"I know."

"Your left eye is swollen half-shut."

"I know."

"And you have a cut on your lip the size of that sinkhole I almost lost you in."

"I know."

"And I want to kiss you so badly I don't think I can stand it, but I'm afraid I'll hurt you if I do."

"Gabriel, I've been hurt so much…so much," she whispered against his shoulder. The one that wasn't injured. "I think the only thing that won't hurt me is a kiss from you."

"You're an amazing woman, Dr. Arabella Burke," he said as he lowered his lips to hers.

It was a gentle kiss, and one that could have had so much more had either of them been in good enough physical condition. But none of that mattered because there, in the middle of the road, when Gabriel kissed Bella, the earth moved again. And this time it wasn't the earthquake.

CHAPTER SEVEN

"READY or not, I think it's going to be a long night," Gabriel said on his way past Bella, who was bent over a young girl, examining a wooden splinter half the size of a man's little finger sticking in the calf of her leg.

"Not ready," Bella replied, bracing herself to remove it but handing the forceps over to Gabriel instead.

He took a look, and made it quick. One clean yank and a very pretty brown leg was well on its way to healing. The church had been turned into the hub for all medical activity. Besides that it was now home for the homeless, a meeting place for those looking for others and a spiritual sanctuary for anyone seeking peace. The tiny building was full to bursting and, crowded or not, it was the best they had. "How about you doing triage?" she asked. Meaning he would assess the injuries according to severity and need. "And treat the minor injuries. I'll take anything that's major."

Which turned out to be a broken leg that Bella splinted as best she could with makeshift material. And a broken arm, another improvised splint. Lots of head injuries, none of which were too serious. Cuts that couldn't be stitched for a lack of supplies—her small amount of suture was being saved for the very worst emergencies while she applied tape to injuries that should have been stitched. Hour after hour, people needing medical care trickled in not only from Lado De la Montaña but from other areas.

"I need more room," Gabriel shouted to Bella above the noise in the church. "I've got another ten people outside who really should be bedded down somewhere for a while."

More room? They needed a whole medical clinic, Bella thought as she washed abrasive cinders from the eyes of an older gentleman who'd insisted that she treat everybody else before she got to him. They needed Rosie's medical clinic. "I questioned my sister's motives," she said to the man, who didn't understand a word of English. "Or maybe it was my own motives I questioned. And to be honest, I thought she was crazy for coming back here the way she was going to—just arrive and everything would work out. That's what my sister thought would happen, and others believed her, probably because she believed it so much herself. She was like that. But I was the one who doubted."

"Crazy," he repeated, grinning at her.

"You're right. I was, maybe still am because I thought that I could come here and step into her dream…maybe as a tribute, or to make amends some way. But…"

A gentle hand on her shoulder stopped her confession to a man who, for all she knew, could have thought she was talking about the weather. "It's Marisol Reyes," Gabriel said, as Bella spun around.

"No! She's not…?"

"She's in heavy labor. Father Carlos just wobbled down to her house—I couldn't stop him—and she's having trouble. He said the pains are coming pretty fast. Maybe every minute."

"I don't think she can deliver that baby vaginally, Gabriel. You were there. You know it's huge. Then with the way her blood pressure is elevated…"

"Do you have anything critical going on here?" he asked.

She shook her head.

"Then I think we're going to go deliver a baby together, one way or another. Which I haven't done since I was a resident, by the way." He grabbed hold of Bella's arm and led her through the people clustered everywhere, then out onto the street where there were even more people.

It was an amazing thing, Bella thought. So many of them had lost their homes and everything they owned, yet there wasn't a great sense of panic or urgency. They were milling about like they might have been going to a church social. And they were helping, comforting, reassuring each other. "I don't have anything in my medical bag that's going to do any good delivering a baby," she shouted, running down the road trying to keep up with Gabriel. Nothing to ease the pain of a natural birth, nothing with which to do a Caesarean should that become necessary.

But she had Gabriel, and that made everything better. Bella seconded that feeling the instant they stepped into Marisol's home and saw a woman fully involved in having a baby. She was in bed, three of the village women were standing over her, watching her pant and push. "Tell her not to push," she told Gabriel as she went to the end of the bed and had a look, only to discover that the baby's head was crowning. "It's on the way," she said to Gabriel, who was already assessing Marisol's vital signs.

"Her blood pressure is topping out," Gabriel replied. "One-eighty over one-ten."

"Damn," Bella muttered. "And we don't have anything to control it." She looked at the ladies, who were anxiously engaged in busy work now—fluffing pillows, massaging Marisol's shoulders—then she looked back at Gabriel. "Can you hypnotize her?"

He chuckled. "Those of us who are experienced in the field prefer calling it the progressive relaxation technique."

"Well, I think you'd better start relaxing her, because this baby wants out and it's going to be a hard struggle." Brushing by Gabriel on her way to the kitchen to wash her hands, she stopped for a moment. "I'm glad you're here to do this." His response was drowned out by a moan from Marisol, but Bella didn't need to hear it. She saw the smile on his face, and that was enough.

* * *

"Almost there," Bella said, feeling sweat beading on her brow. "How's her blood pressure?"

Gabriel nodded, indicating that it was not dire. He was still engaged in lulling Marisol into a relaxed state and Bella didn't want to disturb that. If Gabriel kept her blood pressure down, she'd be happy, because all she needed was another minute or two. "Next time the pain comes, give me a good push, Marisol."

Gabriel translated, and Marisol nodded. She was fighting the pain, her face red, her night-gown drenched with sweat, and Bella was still worried. Two minutes was an awfully long time in a difficult birth, and so many things could happen. She was sure Gabriel was thinking about his sister right now.

"Now, Marisol, push…push…hard!"

Marisol pushed, screamed and pushed some more. Naturally her husband, George, chose that moment to enter the house. He took one look at his wife's condition, and at the baby that Bella was turning in order to help it all the way out, and passed out cold on the floor. At that moment the baby let out a wail that was worthy of his very large size, and Marisol collapsed back into her bed in an exhausted heap.

"A good ten pounds, I'll bet," Bella said, as she handed the newborn over to one of the ladies. "And beautiful. Ten fingers, ten toes, and all the right equipment."

"Well, Marisol's still struggling, but she'd holding her own. And the father…" Gabriel glanced down at him. "He'll have one hell of a headache when he comes to." He took Marisol's blood pressure, and gave a big sigh of relief. "It's down to one-fifty over one hundred. How's the baby?"

Bella asked one of the ladies, who informed him that the baby was just fine. She was cleaning up the infant, getting him ready to show to Marisol. "I think he's doing better than either of his parents." She looked over at Gabriel, who seemed far away, distracted. Thinking about his sister. It had to be tough, and her heart did go out to him. "How are you holding up?" she asked.

He frowned for a moment, then nodded. "I'm good." He paused. Thought about it again, then nodded again. "I *am* good," he repeated, this time sounding like he meant it.

"I was worried because—"

"Bringing a new life into the world takes the

sting out of a lot of things. I'm glad we were here to help Marisol through this."

He didn't say the rest of the words, but she knew them. If they hadn't been there, another woman might have died in childbirth because there was no doctor in the village to help. It was a bitter pill to swallow, and Bella felt it in the pit of her stomach. "Me, too," she agreed.

"Like I told you before, we make one hell of a team." And a fast one. From the moment they'd entered the door until now it had been fifteen minutes. Marisol hadn't had much more time left than that, and Gabriel was amazed by the way he and Bella worked so well together, anticipating each other, almost without words between them. It had saved two lives and, for the first time, the thought crossed his mind that they would do well together in a clinic here. If he stayed. Which he wouldn't. But if he did, they could have a hell of a medical practice together.

Could he stay?

Gabriel tried picturing himself giving up the things he'd worked so hard for, the things that defined his life in Chicago, then pushed the thought from his head. Of course he couldn't stay. The emotion of the moment was clouding his judgment. That's all it was. Different emotions, different worlds, different everything. He was only reacting to his sister's death. That was all it could be.

George Gabriel Reyes had been in the world all of thirty minutes now, most of it spent with his father sitting in a chair, holding an ice pack on his head, while his mother reclined in bed, smiling, holding on to him. Bella was busy fussing over mother and baby while Gabriel stood back and watched her. She was an amazing lady, an amazing doctor. Totally out of her element here, yet she didn't let that stop her from doing anything. And the thing that amazed him most—the sadness was gone from her eyes. When she found herself in her work, the sadness vanished. Bella was finding her heart here in the village, with her work, and he was happy for her. But sad for himself because those thoughts he'd had about the two of them meeting for long weekends halfway between Chicago and San Francisco would never be anything more than thoughts. "I need to get back to the church," he finally said, even though he didn't want to leave Bella. "Who knows what we've got going on over there? I think one of us should be there."

"I'd like to stay here a little while longer, just to keep an eye on George Gabriel. He's doing well, but I just want to make sure no complications set in. So I'll be along in an hour or so. And if you need me in the meantime, send someone to get me."

Before he walked out the door, Gabriel went over to Bella and pulled her into his arms. "It's been quite a day, hasn't it?"

"Quite a day," she whispered.

"How about the two of us finding a bed and grabbing a couple of hours' sleep when you get back to the church?"

"Why, Dr. Velascos, that almost sounds like a proposition."

"If I weren't so tired, it might have been. But the only rise I'm capable of right now is my chest going up and down, hopefully while I'm in a horizontal position." The sad thing was, he meant it. But the thought of curling up with Bella, if only to sleep, had almost as much appeal as curling up with her for other purposes.

"Then I'd say it's a date. I'll see you in an hour if everything goes well."

An hour that was going to seem more like an

eternity. "An hour," he said, then brushed her lips with a gentle kiss.

One his way back to the church he really wanted to remind himself that he was playing with dangerous emotions here, that there was no way he and Bella could have anything between them. But he couldn't, and he didn't want to figure out why.

Practically dragging herself through the church's narthex, Bella was greeted by dozens of people all huddled in little groups inside the chapel itself, families and knots of friends claiming specific pews as their random domiciles. Babies were crying. Children whining. Adults talking in animated voices, trying to drown out the other noises. The level of noise in the tiny structure reverberated in Bella's head, caused the dull ache already there to throb even harder.

It wasn't like she didn't want to be around all these people, because she did. They were so gracious in the face of such a large catastrophe that it overwhelmed her. But she needed time to be away from it all. Time to unwind. The quiet time Gabriel had promised her. Which wasn't to be had even in her tiny room, as it had been turned into a nursery for the youngest babies. In total, there were nine of them in there, all nestled into various boxes that had been scrounged, all attended by mothers or other village women who were busy diapering, feeding and rocking.

Immediately, Bella looked for Ana Maria, but couldn't find her.

"Gabriel's gone over to the rectory," Father Carlos said. "Which is where you need to go, too. We need you both to stay well so you can help us through this. Oh, and he took the baby with him, and I believe they've gone to *my* room."

Gabriel had taken Ana Maria with him. That made her feel good. Even a little warm and mushy, considering the hard shell he'd put on about the baby at first. "Then you know where I'll be," she said. "And if anything comes up…" Before her last words were out, the father shooed her out the side door to the chapel, the one with the portico leading straight into the small rectory. "You have yourself a good rest, Bella," he called after her. "It's a blessing for us that you were here at the time we needed you. A blessing, and a miracle."

"A blessing maybe, but there aren't any

miracles, Father," she said, as she stopped long enough to have a look out over the village. It was getting dark now, and even the fading evening light couldn't hide all the destruction here. What had been so vibrant when she'd woken up that morning was gone. Vanished, in the blink of an eye.

Like her sister.

Sighing under the weight of the world on her shoulders, Bella shook her head. "No miracles anywhere," she whispered.

"I understand that your heart is broken, Bella, but I promise that if you allow it to happen, it *will* heal in time. You will find what you need to heal it when you most need it, and with that you'll also discover there are miracles everywhere. All you have to do is look around and open your entire essence to them."

How could he even think such a thing? After a long day of earthquakes and aftershocks, and with nearly half of Lado De la Montaña in ruins, how could anybody...even a priest... look for miracles here? Certainly, she admired him for his optimism because when all else failed, being optimistic went a long way. But she didn't share it. "I think I must see something different than you do when I look around because I don't see any miracles anywhere."

"You saw George Gabriel Reyes today, didn't you?"

Bella laughed. "You don't give up, do you?"

"Go to the rectory. Take care of yourself," the priest said, then winked. "And Gabriel. Take care of him, too. He's part of that miracle you're not ready to see yet."

"You take care of yourself too, Father," she said. "Get that rest I prescribed hours ago because the people here need you…need your optimism." That included her. And for the first time since she couldn't remember when, she thought she actually felt a little of it.

There were several people inside the priest's house when she stepped in the door, people who'd taken refuge there, but Bella found Gabriel alone, in the tiny bedroom at the back where Father Carlos had said he'd be. The door was closed, separating Gabriel from the dozen or so other people there, and when she went in, he was stretched out on the bed, holding Ana Maria. It was a picture-postcard scene, with the baby sound asleep against his chest, all nuzzled into his cotton T-shirt as if she didn't have a care in the world. Gabriel wasn't sleeping, though. His eyes were open, and even in the dim light of the kerosene lamp Bella could see that he was simply staring at the ceiling. "Can I come in?"

"You know don't have to ask, Arabella," he said, very quietly. Then he scooted over in the single bed, moving himself as close to the wall as he could get, until his injured shoulder was touching it. "There's not much room here, but you're welcome to share it with us."

It didn't take a second invitation for her to crawl in next to him and, right away, she was making herself comfortable in the creaky old bed. "How are you?" she whispered.

"Tired, but good. Most of the people I've been treating are in about the same condition I'm in. Minor injuries, a few major ones like broken bones, that we'll eventually have to get out of here for proper treatment. Nothing critical, though. And you?"

"Tired, but good, too. Marisol and her family are doing well, and the ladies promised to stay there with them for the rest of the night. We're beginning to get more and more people wandering in from other villages and I actually saw a couple of them on my way over here. They've heard the doctors are here…"

"Doctors without supplies. This is crazy, Arabella. We need—"

"Everything. I know, and, believe me, I've been trying to think of a way to get in touch with someone…anyone. But we're so cut off right now. Although Father Carlos did say he's trying to reach Father Frank Marcos, an old friend of mine in San Francisco, by shortwave radio. Apparently he has one in the church. In the meantime, I've sent two men off to Iquitos. They may have to walk a good bit of the way to get past that hole in the road and its not going to be easy doing it in the dark, but maybe somewhere farther down the mountain they'll be able to find someone to help us." She reached over and laid a hand on Ana Maria's back, just from the pure need to touch something so unaffected by all the tragedy and uncertainty encircling them. "It's amazing, isn't it? All's right with her world because the person she trusts most is here to protect her. For her, it's just that simple. And she senses that protection, you know. Babies are so aware…maybe more aware of things than we are."

"Do you really believe that?" he asked.

"More than believe it. I know it. Babies come from a relatively safe world inside their mothers into this strange new place where they're totally helpless, one of most helpless infants of all species, and all they have to rely on are their instincts." Bella twisted to her left side, pressing herself even harder to Gabriel. Ana Maria felt protected there, and so did she. It was a feeling she hadn't expected to find here, in this place so near where her sister had died. It was a feeling she hadn't expected to find ever again. But in the span of only a few short days so much had changed in her life. Different outlook and different sensibilities, and…Gabriel.

It wasn't time to admit her true feelings for him because there was the possibility that proximity and circumstances were causing what she thought was happening to her…those strange, stray emotions she tried to fight off. And was failing so miserably at doing now. This could all be a matter of her needing someone now that she didn't have Rosie, and Gabriel was there, convenient for her. That was a definite possibility. But so was falling in love with him. It was bad timing, though. Really bad timing when nothing was normal and everything was so confusing. No time to think, no time to pose the arguments with herself. "My sister died on this mountain," she said, surprised how easily it had come.

"That's right. You started to mention your sister just before the earthquake. Was she one of the medical group coming here?"

"A nurse. It was her medical group, actually. She was the one who was fighting so hard to set up a clinic here."

"Arabella, I'm so sorry," he whispered. "I knew that you were connected to them somehow, but I never guessed how deeply, and I'm so sorry for your loss."

It felt so strange, telling him. "When we first met, Gabriel, there was no need to tell you. You were merely a stranger who needed help with a baby, and I happened to be particularly good at caring for babies. But then when you came here and we became…friends, and after I found out that your sister had just died…I couldn't tell you, Gabriel. Your sister's death, my sister's death…what would have been the point? You had your own tragedy to suffer and I had… That's the thing. I had nothing. When all the searchers were here, looking for the airplane, and all the families of the people on board came down, just to be closer…I didn't. I couldn't. I simply…went back to work. And that's what I did when the searchers gave up their hunt and all the families huddled together, mourning their losses. I worked. And here you were, doing the right thing by your family and the people who loved Lynda.

"There was a memorial service, Gabriel, for my friends. For Rosie, and I…" She swiped angrily at a tear trickling down her cheek, the saltiness of it stinging the cuts and scrapes there. "She was all I had in the world. It was just the two of us, no parents, and all I did was…"

"The best you could do," he whispered. "You did the best you could do. In the end, that's all any of us can do, Arabella."

"No one thought so, though. Not my friends, not my co-workers. They all thought I was cold, indifferent. Or having a mental breakdown because I wasn't investing all the same emotion the others were showing. But I was. My heart was breaking and I was doing the one thing I knew would get me through it, because if I didn't…"

Gabriel shifted position as Ana Maria snuggled

into him a little more. "There's no instruction book telling us how we're supposed to act in difficult situations, Arabella. Truth is, we all act, and react, differently. Do the best we can, I suppose. I mean, I wasn't exactly great about Lynda. My immediate reaction was more about being inconvenienced by her child. I looked for excuses, I avoided… You were there. You saw me—you know."

"What I know is that you came here right away, and did everything right when you had to. You took care of Ana Maria, and helped your mother. You've been the support she needed."

"On my own terms."

Bella laid a gentle hand on his arm. "Changing your life isn't easy. I've had to do that a few times in my life and sometimes you can't be as gracious about it as you want to be. But that's understandable."

"And you're about to change your life again, aren't you?"

"I think so." She liked it here, liked being needed. Liked taking care of the people. More than that, she felt like she could belong, be part of Rosie's dream. Or maybe, *finally*, have a dream of her own. "But, like I said, it's not easy."

"No, it's not. When my mother told me I would have to raise Ana Maria, I argued with her. My very first thoughts were how she wasn't going to fit into my life." He ran a gentle hand over the baby's back and it was like a sense of peace, and purpose, came over him. "I should have been thinking about how she'd lost her mother and her father, and how that would affect her life, but I was thinking about myself. I didn't want her and, to be honest with you, after the nurse from the adoption agency approached me, there was a moment or two when I thought that might be a good decision. To find a nice home for her with people who really wanted a daughter. Give away my own flesh and blood."

"But the thing is, that thought lasted only a moment or two. It was a reaction to a situation, Gabriel, not a real thought or plan. My sister and my friends died weeks ago, and I'm only now coming here to face this. Only now having my own reactions."

"Like I said, we do the best we can, Arabella. That's all we can do, and I know you didn't grieve any less for not coming here with the others. Being by yourself through it could have been harder, could have made you grieve even more because you didn't get that support everyone else had. My mother and I…we have that, and I don't even want to think what it would be like going through Lynda's death alone."

"And I'm just the opposite. I couldn't imagine what it would be like going through Rosie's death with so many people around me. So I didn't because I've never had support other than my sister's and I didn't know how. It was, like, if I did all those things everybody else did, I wouldn't have Rosie any more."

Gabriel shifted slightly, taking Bella's hand in his, then he raised it to his lips and kissed it. "She sounds like she was an amazing woman. Was Rosie as dedicated to her medical work as you?"

She hadn't talked about her sister, not in any real sense, since the accident, yet this seemed so right. Like it was time, and Gabriel was the one meant to listen. "More dedicated. She was the best nurse…the one who inspired me to go into medicine in the first place. Rosie always wanted to be a nurse, and she'd talked about it from the time we were little. After my parents died there was a great deal of money left in trust for us, so that was never a problem. She wanted to be the nurse, I wanted to be the doctor, and we made plans. Just the two of us together, forever.

"Rosie was amazing. Happy in spite of everything we went through, everything I put her through. Dedicated. The person I most admired in the world." Until she'd met Gabriel.

"It sounds to me like she was a woman who would have wanted her sister staying back and taking care of children who needed her rather than spending that time in a futile pursuit, huddling around with a bunch of strangers waiting for, as it turned out, nothing. Am I right?"

Odd he would say that, because that sounded just like Rosie. *Do something that counts, Bella. That's what will always make you happiest.* "You are. She was just like that," Bella whispered. "She was everything that I'm not."

"I don't believe that. Not for a minute. From the way you talk about her, and from what I've seen in you, I think your sister was every good thing that you are, and you are every good thing she was. You're too overwhelmed with grief right now to recognize that, though. You can't see past that grief to find what's on the other side—and there is another side, Arabella." He stroked Ana Maria's head. "I promise. There really is another side…a better side, when you finally let yourself see it."

Bella couldn't respond to that, couldn't find the words. Maybe there wasn't anything to say, or maybe she simply didn't know how to take Gabriel's words to heart yet. Whatever the case, she tucked her head into Gabriel and shut her eyes. A few minutes later, as she drifted off to sleep, so physically tired and so emotionally raw she was pretty sure she knew the answer to one of her questions. *This was the man she loved.* The only man she'd ever loved. She wasn't ready for it, and the time wasn't right. This was the first time she'd ever wondered if there could be a time for it, however. The very first time in her life, as the tiniest spark of hope ignited deep inside her. It was enough for now. Better than she'd expected. More than she deserved. "Thank you," she whispered as a wave of sleep washed her away on its tide. A pleasant, gentle tide, for once.

"I hate to disturb you…" Father Carlos poked his head in the door, keeping his eyes squeezed tightly shut. "Juan Gabriel, Bella, we have a situation…not so good, I'm afraid. I need a doctor. Either one of you. And quickly."

Instantly, Bella sat up, as did Gabriel, who startled Ana Maria wide awake, and that's when the screaming began. "Let me go and find my mother to take care of the baby," Gabriel began, but Bella was already out of bed, quite surprised that she'd slept for nearly two hours—slept deeply, no disturbing dreams.

It was amazing what a nap could do to make a body feel better, because hers did. She felt like she'd slept a full night. Or maybe she felt better due to all the things Gabriel had said before her nap. She may have heard those things before from other people…she didn't remember, but she'd needed to hear them from him for them to make any sense. The reconciliation wasn't lodged fully in her heart yet, and might never be, but on another level she knew he was right in some ways. There really was another side for her, when she was ready to see it. The question was, would she ever be ready? "I'll go," Bella volunteered to the priest, who immediately trotted out of the room. She turned to Gabriel, who was sitting up now, trying to quieten Ana Maria. "You take care of her and I'll meet you back in the church in a little while. Maybe we can figure out what we need to do next." Medically speaking. Not romantically because, for all practical purposes, that couldn't happen, even though she thought it would be so easy. And nice.

"Next, for me, is a diaper change," he said, turning up his nose. "That's the one part of this whole parental responsibility thing I don't like so much."

Bella laughed. "Says the surgeon, who has no problem cutting people open."

"That's different."

He looked so adorable, so helpless and adorable, she couldn't help herself. Before she left the room, Bella bent over the bed and first kissed Ana Maria, then kissed Gabriel tenderly on the lips. It was a lingering kiss, not so much in duration as it was in the way it made her feel afterward. It was as if she'd waited a lifetime for Gabriel's kiss. Who knows? Maybe she had. "You'll do fine." She hated pulling away from him then dashing from the room, but she had to. Duty called.

"They found Natali Diego still in her house just a little while ago. She's not good," Father Carlos called back over his shoulder once Bella had caught up with him. He was winded, his voice filled with exhaustion and rough emotion as they ran along the dark trail to a house that sat just a short way away from the main road through the village. "When some of the men went there earlier to see if anybody was in the house, they didn't find her, and assumed she'd gone to shelter, like so many of the people were doing. But later, when we started making a list of everybody in the village, and realized nobody had seen Natali, some of the men went back to her house and found her hiding in the closet, holding little Miguel. Protecting him." His voice cracked, and he cleared his throat. "When they looked at her she was not so good. We decided not to move her out of there until you or Juan Gabriel took a look."

They'd been lucky in Lado De la Montaña so far. No deaths, no serious injuries. But the people here were of hearty stock and while a few of them would be laid up awhile recovering, the worst of the damage had been to the buildings. Everything considered, it could have been much worse, and she only hoped some of that luck had rubbed off on Natali Diego and little Miguel. Judging from the sound of the priest's voice, though, she wasn't very optimistic about that.

Father Carlos led Bella through the door of

the tiny one-room home. "Sorry it's dark in here. But we do have a few lanterns." He gestured for three men standing around the edges of the room with lit lanterns to move in closer. Grimness distorted their faces in the glow given off from the flames.

"How's the boy?" she asked, rushing over to the man who held him. Miguel was sniffling, and scared in a way no child that age should ever be scared, but a quick exam satisfied Bella that, other than a few scrapes, he was fine. So she turned her attention to Miguel's mother. "Where's the closet?"

One of the man pointed to the closet door, a wooden structure that looked just like the room's walls. Rough-hewn boards. An undersized door, at that. And, sure enough, Natali was lying in there, wedged into an odd angle and almost hunched over and kneeling—to protect her child, Bella guessed, a child now in the arms of one of the men.

Part of the exterior wall had collapsed from the outside, on top of her, effectively pinning her under a pile of debris. The men had pulled back the wood as best they could from the outside wall and, in essence, Bella was looking at the dark of the night through what was more hole than wall. "Natali," she said, dropping to her knees, wondering why the woman hadn't tried getting herself out of the closet after the quakes had ended. "My name is Bella, and I'm a doctor."

She tried extending her hand to feel for a pulse, but found the woman nearly impossible to reach so she scrambled to her feet, ran outside and tried again from the hole in the exterior wall. And that's when she saw what made her sick to her stomach. Natali's back was nearly snapped in half, in two different places. Her spine was zigzagged at such odd angles... horrible angles. Fatal angles. The woman had taken her child to the closet when the earthquake had hit, thinking it was the safest place, and had literally used her own body to protect him. Which had cost her everything.

"Natali," she said, gently, laying fingers over a very weak pulse in the woman's neck. "Miguel is fine. We have him out of the closet, and he's with Father Carlos right now. You did a good job protecting him. He's safe now, Natali. He's safe and he's not injured." It's what a dying mother would want to hear, she thought. To give your life for your child, as Natali had done, yes, this was what she would want to hear. "You can rest now, Natali. Miguel is well and we will take care of him for you. You can let go."

"Can we help you bring her out?" Father Carlos asked from the other side of the closet. He shone a light in Bella's face, and her expression was all the answer he needed. "Can she hear me?"

"I think so."

"Can I get closer to her from where you are?"

"A little." Natali's pulse was going thready. Skipping beats. She was sliding from this life now that she knew her son was safe. It was a mother's last act of love, staying with her child as long as she could. How she must love her little boy, Bella thought as she took Natali's hand in hers and held it.

Father Carlos ran around to the hole on the exterior and huddled into the closet interior, pressing himself up against Bella, performing the sacred duties to which he was entrusted at the end of a life. And that life ended before his words ran out. When Bella next felt for Natali's pulse, it flickered away under her fingertips, and Natali let out her last breath. In that hollow fraction of a moment that came between life and death, a cold chill swept over Bella. It always did, and she thought about Rosie. "I'm sorry I couldn't do anything for her," Bella said, brushing back tears. "She was only waiting to know that her son was safe before she went."

"No greater sacrifice," Father Carlos replied, laying a gentle hand atop Bella's. "The love only a mother could have for her child."

"Only a mother, or a father." Bella sniffled again, her thoughts now turning to Gabriel and Ana Maria. He loved that child, probably more than he knew. He would have done the same. Of that, she had no doubt. "So, let me go have a better look at Miguel now. And maybe you should go find the boy's father, let him know…"

"No father. Natali was only sixteen. I met her in Andoas a few months ago, when I went to visit an old friend. I brought her here as a favor to her parents. They wanted her to learn responsibility by working on one of the farms down in the flatlands."

"Then I think they'd be proud," Bella whispered. "Will they take Miguel?"

Father Carlos nodded. "They'll do the right thing."

"It's a miracle he survived," she whispered, as she went to check the boy.

"Says the doctor who doesn't believe in miracles." Father Carlos gave her a kind smile. "I think you've had a change of heart?"

"Well, maybe there are miracles, but they're always surrounded by so much sadness. Miracles and sadness." Her own parents had been killed in the car wreck, yet she and her sister, both of them strapped into the backseat, had barely even been scratched. The sadness part of it she understood in so many painful ways, but the miracles she didn't. Maybe that was due to the words she'd heard so often after their accident—*It's a miracle*. Even at the tender age of five, she had known enough to understand that a miracle was a good thing. But she never felt good about her so-called miracle, and every time she heard the word, all it did was make her ache all the more. She might have been the miracle, but her parents were dead, which made the miracle unbearable. Which turned the miracle into the sadness.

So Miguel was the miracle. But at such a high price. That was the sadness he would have to face when he was older. And she felt that old, familiar ache for him.

"And who do we have here?" Gabriel asked, as Bella carried the boy into the church. All eyes went to her as she shifted Miguel, who was trying to reach out to Gabriel, to her other hip. "His name is Miguel Diego and I don't know much about him except that he's in good condition."

"His family?" Gabriel asked.

Bella shook her head. "His mother stayed with him long enough to make sure he was safe, then she…" She wouldn't say the word. While Miguel didn't speak English, and wouldn't understand what she was saying even if he did, she simply couldn't utter the dreadful words around him. "Father Carlos is taking care of the arrangements, contacting his family, and for the time being, I think we have a young man to look after."

"Are you OK?" Gabriel asked, his voice so gentle she nearly melted from it. When he reached out and stroked her cheek, she did melt, right into his embrace. "I couldn't do anything," she choked. "All she wanted was to make sure her baby was safe, that someone would take care of him, and when she knew that had happened, she just… She protected him, Gabriel. With everything she had, she took care of her little boy, and now…" She would have dabbed at the tears streaming down her cheeks but with her arms full of a rowdy little boy who desperately wanted to be put down so he could go play with the other children, she couldn't. So she let the tears soak into Gabriel's shirt.

"You need to rest," he said. "A little while to yourself."

"I need to work."

"That's how you avoid it, isn't it? You work rather than giving in to what you're feeling. You work to avoid your feelings, to avoid the grief, and that's not good. Sometimes we need to welcome the pain in before we can start to heal from it."

"I work because I have to. It's the only thing I know how to do, the only thing that doesn't let me down."

"Arabella, have you ever allowed yourself to feel the things you want to, or need to? Or do you always bury so much of yourself away?"

"It's safer," she admitted. "And easier."

"But is it really? Right now the only thing you want to do is stay here and mother that little boy, and that's admirable. Yet you won't admit it, and, to make matters worse, you've got your strong sense of duty to hide behind. Who would ever question a doctor who's doing his or her duty? People will remark about the sacrifices you make, tell you how it's a wonderful thing that you devote your life to your work, yet they'll never ask why you have nothing left over for yourself. And that's the question I'm asking, Arabella. Why do you want nothing for yourself?"

Bella pulled out of Gabriel's arms and reared back. "What I want of myself is to be the best doctor I can be. That's all, and it's enough, even if you don't think so. I don't need anything else to validate myself to me, or prove myself to others, or make me happy."

"What terrible things are you paying penance for?" he asked, reaching over to pull her back to him. But she stepped backward, then handed Miguel to one of the women helping with all the children, who took him straight away to the area set off to feed the little ones. Bella watched until Miguel was eating a tortilla before she looked at Gabriel again.

"You call it penance, I call it doing what I want to do." So much guilt defied an explanation. No one could understand. And why should they have to? It was her life to live, her guilt to carry. No one else need be involved. "Which is being a doctor."

"A doctor bordering on obsession?"

"Not obsession, Gabriel. And even if it were, would it really matter so much to you?"

"Yes," he said simply. "It would matter."

That surprised her. As many barriers as she erected, he just seemed to knock them down. Another time, another place it would have been different. They wouldn't have been thrown into the close proximity, fighting so many battles shoulder to shoulder. Then she wouldn't be so attracted to him, and he wouldn't feel so obligated to take care of her. Simple as that. "Well, don't. Because it won't get you anywhere. I don't get involved."

"That's not true. You get involved more than anybody I've ever seen, but you do a damn fine job of covering it up. And I'm not sure if you're hiding it from others, or from yourself."

"I have patients to see," she said stiffly. OK, so maybe he was right about *some* things. She *was* a little obsessed sometimes, and she did tend to get more involved than she should. But that involved only her, which was the way she intended on keeping it. "Even more villagers are wandering in now, and by morning we're going to be overcrowded. So I need to see as many of them as I can before the sun comes up." Which was still a good eleven hours away.

"Then I'll help you."

"What about Ana Maria…"

"With my mother." He smiled gently. "I'm not going to let you push me away, Arabella. To begin with, I want to be with you while we're working to get through this crisis. But apart with that, I want to be with you…"

"No! Don't say that." It was what she wanted to hear more than anything else in her life, but it was the one thing she couldn't hear. Wouldn't hear. Especially now that she was sure she was in love with Gabriel.

"It'll keep," he said. "For now. But you have to know, it won't go away just because you wish it away."

Wishes, like miracles, were things that let you down. It would have been nice if she could have believed, though. Never in her life had she wanted anything so desperately as she did Gabriel. But she knew better, and that's why she had to rely on the one thing she trusted most—her work. At the end of the day, that's all there was.

CHAPTER EIGHT

IT HAD been twenty-four hours since the first earthquake, and Bella was convinced, finally, that the worst of the medical duty was over. Stragglers from other villages were still coming in, but not in the droves of twelve hours earlier, and most of the injuries were minor now. Cuts, scrapes, reactions to fear. She and Gabriel had a small amount of medical supplies available to them now, too. A few odds and ends had been dropped in by helicopter several hours ago, along with some food staples, thanks to Father Carlos's shortwave relay from Lado De la Montaña to who knew where?

The village itself was still pretty much cut off from anything down the nearest side of the mountain, unless the desire for escape and a good long hike became overwhelming, but that was fine with Bella. She had no reason to go anywhere.

Men were working to fill the giant sinkhole in

the road and, overall, needs were being met. People were rebounding, they were digging around in the ruins for personal possessions, and even making plans to rebuild.

Finally, now that she had a chance to relax a little, Bella's weariness was sinking in, the aches and pains of hard physical work catching up with her. But it was a good kind of tired. With so much potential for horrible things to have happened from the earthquake, there'd only been one fatality. One was never good, and it was so sad that such a young life had been taken. Though after everything she'd seen these past hours, she knew that Lado De la Montaña had been spared untold tragedy and suffering. Material objects could be replaced, houses rebuilt. But with so few lives destroyed here, she almost had to believe that some kind of miracle had taken place. *Almost.*

"How's Ana Maria?" she asked Gabriel, who was about to stretch out in bed with her. It was amazing how much she missed her…even more amazing how quickly she'd gotten used to seeing her, and loved watching the little changes that took place day by day. It was as if a quick peek at Ana Maria just made things better, and she envied Gabriel a lifetime of that.

Bella had her little room in the back of the church all to herself now. The chapel part was still full to overflowing with people who'd lost homes and would have no place to go for some time to come. Father Carlos, bless his heart, had shooed away the people occupying her room, telling them the doctor needed rest. Which was true. She did.

"My mother took her to stay with one of her cousins, who lives in a little village just south of here. The road has easy access, and until I can manage to have her home rebuilt, I thought it would be best to keep both of them away from all this. Besides, they're with family, which is good."

"Your mother will stay here, in Lado De la Montaña?"

"She's being stubborn about it, telling me this is her home, no matter what shape it's in, that she's not going anywhere." He shook his head, and gave her a playful wink. "Stubborn women. The bane of my existence. Let's hope Ana Maria turns out better."

"You're going to spoil her rotten, you know."

"That's your prediction?"

"A single father raising a little girl? I'd say it's inevitable. One look at you with those big, brown eyes of hers and you're going to be totally lost."

"She is pretty, isn't she?" He said that almost timidly, like he wanted to brag but didn't know if he should. "I thought maybe I was a little partial since, as a rule, I don't think most newborns are very pretty."

"You don't?" Actually, that was a familiar comment she heard from many new fathers... *Will my baby get prettier?* That said while trying to hide his turned-up nose from the adoring new mother who could see nothing but beauty in her child.

"You do?"

"Of course I do! Newborns have a unique beauty. And they have the most amazing baby smell..." That was the woman in her talking, not the doctor. "Then there's the way they scrunch up their little faces and cry..."

"You should have children, Arabella. Lots and lots of newborns."

Was he being sarcastic about that? Because she wanted children. Lots and lots of them, as he'd just said. But that required a commitment she just wouldn't make. And a man, which she just couldn't have...at least, not until her life was sorted out. "When I'm practicing in pediatrics, I have lots and lots of children," she said, her voice edgy. Why did it always get back to something she couldn't have? Why were the nice moments ruined by the realities? "So, you're sure you can't convince your mother to go back to Chicago with you, at least for a little while?" she asked, deliberately and not so delicately changing the subject. "I'd think she'd love the chance to be there with the two of you, watching her only granddaughter grow up."

"Home is where the heart is, and you can't fight the heart. This is where my mother's heart is."

But not his? That caused a dull ache to well up in her, because in the back of her mind she'd wondered if he *could* stay. She'd allowed herself to dream into the future, with the two of them working together in a little clinic here. But now she had her answer. To be honest, it didn't surprise her. In so many ways, Gabriel was as connected to his work as she was to hers. He didn't see that, though. So, while she wasn't surprised he wouldn't stay, she *was* surprised by how disappointed she felt. "Be it ever so humble." Bella's words tumbled out on a sigh. "So, how long before you'll be going back to Chicago?"

"Not for a while yet. I've got to take care of my mother one way or another, and I think the village is going to need both of us here to do the doctoring for a little while longer. A couple of weeks, I suppose. I mean, at some point I've got to figure out how Ana Maria and I are going to make a go of it together in our new life. You know, figuring out schedules and routines, those kinds of things. It's going to be an adjustment, and I haven't really given it much thought, but it's going to happen sooner or later, no matter how many ways I put it off. So I think we'll probably just rip the sticky bandage off the cut as soon as possible and get the initial shock of it over with."

It all sounded so easy when he talked about it but, in reality, it scared him thinking about how many ways he could mess this up. To be honest, he'd pictured himself staying here in Lado De la Montaña, opening up a clinic with Arabella. The fantasy of a cozy little family of three had such a wonderful appeal he could almost feel it, but it was just another avoidance. He'd become so good at it that it was sneaking up on him now, pelting him in ways he didn't even recognize. And this little fantasy was one of those ways. It sounded ideal but when he got down to the hard thinking, it was something he'd never wanted. Which could only mean that the reason he wanted it now was for the convenience of having Arabella nearby to bail him out when it came to Ana Maria, the way she had so many times already. And if not her, then his mother.

He wasn't proud of feeling that way, but it was the only thing that made sense to him when his thoughts turned to how nice it might be if he stayed.

"So, why didn't you come back here after medical school? You know, return home and do the things you'd probably planned on doing when you left. I mean, that's what so many doctors do, isn't it? Go to medical school with the plan to return home and practice. Then they get distracted, or lured away. That *is* what happened to you, isn't it?"

He pulled her into him until she rested her head on his chest, then he wrapped his arms around her. Such a natural fit. One like nothing he'd ever felt before. "You think you know so much about me," he said on a contented sigh.

"Do I?" she teased.

"OK, you're right," he said, chuckling. "I got

sidetracked. I'll admit that, for someone who grew up here, going to a big city like Chicago was overwhelming. But I loved it. Loved the sense of who I was there. I served my residency in the public hospital, worked in a charity clinic, did pretty much the same things there I'd intended doing here, except for the surgery, and that was probably my biggest lure. I really hadn't expected to be a surgeon. For me the dream was always general medicine, and maybe that's because my experience with doctors was so limited. But when I was a student, the first time I held that scalpel in my hand…the rest, as they say, is history. I loved it. It's all I wanted to do. And my history was easier to accomplish in a large hospital, especially at the start of my career. To make a long story short, I made my medical contacts in Chicago, got noticed there by the people who could help my career, had some amazing offers to stay and there was no reason to go anywhere else."

"So you're locked into a big city surgical practice? As in it's your life, non-negotiable?"

"I think the one thing I've learned over the years is that I'm locked into whatever makes me happiest. Sometimes, when I come home, I do think that could be Peru again. I don't realize how much I miss it until I come back here. But then when I get back to Chicago that's what makes me happiest. So, what about you? Is San Francisco your home, or just the city that lured you?"

"No, home, actually. My sister and I were raised by a guardian who felt obligated to look after us because he executed my parents' will. He moved around quite often, and we went with him."

"Was it a good life?" he asked, suddenly serious. "Did you have a happy childhood? Did you get to do the things all little girls should be doing? You know, playing with dolls, trying on make-up?"

"Sometimes, but not too often. We were expected to be proper all the time and, to be honest, he left us with hired caregivers as much as he could, until he sent us off to boarding school. But I never liked dolls, unless I pretended they were sick, then I got to bandage them and give them candy pills and make them better."

"So you were medical from the beginning?"

"Rosie and I both were. I think that kept us connected to our parents. They were both doctors—my mother an anesthesiologist, my father a cardiac surgeon. So maybe the interest was natural inclination, or it could have been our way of trying to keep them in our lives since we really didn't have anyone else."

"What about your guardian?"

Bella let out a ragged breath. "He was my father's business partner, a cardiac surgeon, too. And he was a very… impatient man. He was older, didn't have much time for children, but for some strange reason he'd agreed to serve as our guardian in the event of our parents' deaths. I guess he didn't expect that to happen. But I've always thought it was about his own self-interest, too. He and my father were two of the three major owners of a hospital, and my father's part of the hospital was willed to Rosie and me. So, by keeping an eye on us, our guardian was keeping our share in the hospital under his control. And don't get me wrong. He wasn't a bad man. He handled our affairs honestly, and in our best interests. But handling our affairs and handling us were two different things, and he was much better with the affairs."

"It sounds gloomy. I mean, you can guess the kind of childhood I had here in Lado De la Montaña. It was amazing."

"Well, let's just say that I didn't help matters

any. Dr. Gentry, our guardian…we were never allowed to call him anything else…he and I didn't get along. I had a way of being disruptive. I looked for ways to do things he didn't want us to do. Bad things. Destructive things. In fact, I went out of my way to look for trouble."

"I can't picture you ever being bad. Mischievous maybe, but never bad."

"I was bad, Gabriel. Believe me, I broke things…things I knew Dr. Gentry cared about, like his treasured possessions and valuables. I set little fires in trash cans, called people names, hit other children. Stole little items from the grocery store…packages of gum, candy bars. Once I threw a rock through a plate-glass window just so I could watch it break. And the list is longer than that. I was sullen, angry. I had temper tantrums all the time."

"Dear God, Arabella, didn't this Dr. Gentry ever get you help? You sound like you were a child in need."

"His idea of help was sending me away to a boarding school. Of course, I managed to get myself kicked out."

"And Rosie?"

"He never separated us. He always said that

Rosie was a lovely child who didn't deserve to be punished for the things I did, and that I was the child from hell who would have been a heart-ache to my parents. But when he sent me away, Rosie always fought him to go with me, then he'd tell me that I was the one who held her back and ruined her life. He called me a selfish little girl who didn't deserve the nice sister I had."

"But your sister loved you, and stayed with you. You said she fought to stay with you."

"She was seven years older, and she felt responsible for me. That's what it was. Rosie's obligation to take care of her little sister."

"She took care of you because she loved you, Arabella," he insisted. "And you've never let yourself believe that, have you? Because someone who should have cared about you said bad things, you've never let yourself believe it."

"What I think, Gabriel, is that Dr. Gentry was right about everything he accused me of, no matter how Rosie felt about me. She spent her whole life looking after me, then in the end… look what I did to her." The tears started to slide down her face. "Just look what I did."

"What you did was turn yourself into a mar-velous doctor who's filled with so much compassion you can't contain it. You became a woman who would sacrifice everything to take care of children who need her. It's a fitting legacy for your sister, Arabella. And for your mother and father. Not something that should fill you with so much guilt."

"She never had much of a life, looking after me. Then when she was finally happy…happy in a life where she didn't have to spend so much time trying to fix all the things her sister broke along the way…I let her down. I told her that the way she was going about this was all wrong. We argued for weeks because I just couldn't see how she could take everything she had and turn it into something so…so unknown without having some kind of plan first. It was so risky. She told me, *Be spontaneous, Bella. I know that goes against your nature, but be spontaneous with this. Step outside your normal self just this once. Have some fun. Who knows? Maybe something absolutely wonderful will happen when you least expect it.* But I couldn't, Gabriel. I just couldn't."

Shutting her eyes, Bella tried to picture Rosie, and for a fraction of a second her sister's image was lost to her. Her heart lurched in her chest and her breath caught in her throat. But then the image returned…Rosie, who fit her name. "Dr. Gentry always figured that I was just a spoiled child, inherently bad. Rosie kept insisting that wasn't the case, that she thought there might be something wrong with me. She was standing up for me like a parent would do. But nobody would believe her, so one day she took me on a bus and we went to a medical center on the other side of town. We just walked through the emergency room's front door, a seventeen-year-old and her ten-year-old sister. Rosie marched me over to the clerk and said that her sister needed to see someone who could help her. After the clerk gave us a dozen reasons why that wouldn't be happening, Rosie marched me down the hall anyway, and we went into the first empty exam room we found. We waited for hours, until someone realized we were there.

"I didn't get a proper diagnosis that day, but because of Rosie I was started in the right direction. As it turned out, I had a closure disorder…I didn't really think my parents were dead. If I acted up with Dr. Gentry, and didn't let myself get cozy or complacent in his care, someday my own parents would come back for me. I didn't want another home. I wanted my home and I did everything I could to make sure he wouldn't keep me."

"Poor Arabella. No wonder you were a frustrated child. And Dr. Gentry simply saw you as bad?"

"But I *was* bad. Don't you understand that? Even after the child psychologist worked with me, I still had temper issues, created problems."

"You were only a little girl, who eventually got over those temper tantrums, didn't you?"

"Yes, but only because my sister always believed in me, Gabriel. But in those last weeks, before Rosie was to leave for Peru…"

"Weren't you coming with her?"

"I was, but only for a few weeks."

"And she intended on staying?"

Bella nodded, brushing back a tear. "We were still arguing that last day. Not angry so much as just bickering enough that she asked me not to come to Peru with her group right then. She said we needed a break from each other for a little while, and that maybe it would be better if I stayed behind for a couple of weeks to co-ordinate ordering the supplies they would need once they started setting up. She couldn't see my point of view that it would have been better to make plans, lay things out in an orderly fashion before she acted. She didn't know where she would put the clinic, didn't have a building…she just believed that once they all got here it would fall into place. And I…I needed a logical order to it. She was a dream-chaser and I was too grounded to believe that dreams could come true. We didn't have time to make it right, Gabriel. My sister sent me back, and I never saw her again."

"Arabella," he whispered, pulling her tightly into his arms. "In so many ways you're still that wounded little girl your sister dragged into the hospital, aren't you? The wounds really don't heal so easily, and I don't want to say something trite like give it more time. Because time doesn't always make things better. It certainly doesn't heal all wounds."

"I can deal with it," she said, trying to be stiff about it. But it was impossible to be stiff and sniffle at the same time.

"Said with so much conviction. I know you mean what you say, but that's an awfully tough life sentence to put on yourself, isn't it? Isolating yourself as well as carrying your guilt?"

"Not when I have my work, and work's all I need. It takes care of me."

"Dedication is a good thing, Arabella. But when it's for the right reason."

"You're saying that my dedication is for the *wrong* reason?" She bristled, this time succeeding in pushing herself out of his arms and completely away from him.

"You hide in your work, and succeed nicely because you're an excellent doctor. I'm sure you chose pediatrics because you didn't want other children to go undiagnosed, or misunderstood, the way you were. And that's admirable. But your passion for it should be from the heart, and I think it could be, if you'd allow it. You don't allow your heart any passion, though. Not for anyone to see, anyway. It's locked up tight in some logical place, and you still believe you're all those terrible things Dr. Gentry said you were. So you push people away for *their* good. You hide away in a profession you could love passionately but won't because you're afraid it will add to all the hurts of your life. And you've taken on all the blame for your sister's death now. That's a very big burden, Arabella."

Sitting on the side of the bed, her back to him, she didn't get up. Didn't huddle over and cry either. Instead, she sat up straight and let the tears run down her cheeks, unchecked. "I should have hugged her that day. Should have told her I loved her instead of trying to convince her that she needed to slow down and plan what she was going to do before she leapt straight into the middle of it. There were so many things I should have said, but…" Her voice faded. "If you love someone you should tell them every day…tell them ten times a day, a hundred times… They shouldn't ever walk away from you without knowing how you love them. And I should have told her."

"I know," he whispered, scooting over behind her, then sitting up and pulling her into his arms. "When you lose someone you love you're filled with all the things you should have done differently. I keep wondering what might have happened to Lynda if I'd been here. Would I have seen that something was wrong and gotten her help, would I have been able to prevent something? When I talked to her the day before she died she was so happy, then she was…gone. And I've asked myself all the questions, Arabella. But there are no answers. Never will be."

"It hurts so much, Gabriel. I've been wondering if Rosie's last minutes were filled with anger toward me for the way I argued with her, because they shouldn't have been. They should have been filled with excitement and happiness over what she was on her way to do…following her dream. But maybe I put awful thoughts in her head that stayed there for the rest of her life. Maybe I caused her anguish and pain in those last minutes, and if I did…"

"Shh," he said, holding her even closer, wrapping his arms so tightly around her they were practically one. "There's no blame here, Arabella."

"No blame?" She pulled away again, and stood up. Turning to face him, she straightened her shoulders and slapped away the few remaining tears on her face. "Well, that's where you're wrong, Gabriel. I do get the blame. All of it. And if Dr. Gentry were alive today he'd get to call me selfish again, and be right about it, since I'm the one who wouldn't come here with the other families while everybody waited for word from the rescuers. And I'm the one who wouldn't attend a memorial service for the victims, and I'm the one—" she gulped hard "—who refused to put a grave marker on an empty grave. Just like I refused to believe my parents were dead, which was what caused my sister a miserable life."

"Damn," he muttered, jumping to his feet. He went toward her to pull her back into his arms, but she backed away, pressing herself flat against the door. He didn't give up, though. That's what she wanted him to do, and she was so good at pushing and pushing until people did walk away from her. But he wasn't walking anywhere. Not now, and if he had his way about it, not ever. He did love her, every little wounded speck and fiber of her being. On top of that, he was a very patient man, and she was going to need that in him. "Arabella," he said, stepping around behind her, blocking the door so she couldn't get out.

"Just leave me alone, Gabriel. Please. It's better that way."

"That would be the easy thing to do, if I weren't a man in love with the most impossible, the most stubborn woman he's ever met."

"No!" she choked, scooting around him and running back toward the bed just to get away from him. "Don't say that. Please, don't say that!"

"Do you love me, Arabella?" he asked, still holding his place at the door. If he didn't, she would escape, and as vulnerable as she was right now, he was afraid she'd run away from the village. Escape any way she had to, simply to get away from him. And away from her feelings for him.

"This isn't about my feelings for you, or for anybody else."

"I think it is. So answer my question Arabella. Do you love me?"

"It doesn't matter, Gabriel!" she cried. "Can't you understand that? What I feel or don't feel doesn't matter. I'm not leaving here. And you are. So the rest of it doesn't matter."

"Why are you staying?" he asked.

"Because…Rosie saw the need here, and I can fix that. I can do what she wanted to do, and still have my work."

"Do you remember before, Arabella, when I said that dedication is a good thing, but only when it's for the right reason?"

"The right reason is to take care of all the people here. I do have a reason to stay, Gabriel. Maybe it's not your idea of a good reason, but it will take care of me when you return to Chicago, to the things you want from your life. Which is why our feelings for each other don't matter in this. I can't leave and you can't stay. So why tell you that I love you when all it will do is break my heart even more and, in the end, get me nothing?"

It was Gabriel's turn to step away. Because she was right, and it felt like a slap to the face. Somehow he'd envisioned the scene playing out with her in his arms, telling him she'd follow him anywhere. But Arabella had this life plan from which she wasn't going to divert and he had... well, he had his own life plan, didn't he? Or at least the beginning of one since Ana Maria had changed his original course. "I think you love me. And I know you love Ana Maria. You fell in love with her before I did, in fact."

"Which has nothing to do with anything. Especially us together in any way."

"You're frightened of it, aren't you?" It was so pronounced in her eyes he felt a physical ache in his chest. But he could also see the desire there, the longing for things she wanted and didn't think she deserved. Could he break through to that part of her? Find his way in deep enough to help her discover it in herself? "But admitting your feelings shouldn't frighten you. A very wise woman once told me that if you loved someone you should tell them how much a hundred times a day."

"I'm not frightened," she said, trying to sound

defiant. "More like experienced. With enough sense to know that the circumstances in my life don't change no matter what I'm feeling, or not feeling, for someone."

"I suppose you're right. Circumstances won't change if you don't want them to."

"Circumstances like going back to a medical practice in Chicago no matter what?"

"Or staying in a tiny mountain village in Peru for the wrong reasons, no matter what." Perhaps that was being a little cruel but, damn it, he was frustrated—not only for himself and his inability to simply take the woman he loved into his arms and make it all better for her but with Bella herself, for finding such a complacent spot in the middle of so much unhappiness in her life and simply staying there when he knew she didn't want to. She should be punching her way out of it, and he wanted to help her do it. But how could he even begin to think of a life for himself and Ana Maria with someone who was building her own life simply to assuage guilt? If her reason for staying here and starting a clinic had been about her own passion…well, Chicago might have lost some of its appeal. But there was too much risk involved in planning a future with someone whose only motivation in life was guilt. He was a father now, and he had a little girl who deserved more stability than that. "You're a strong woman, Arabella. You can change the things in your life you don't like." He laid his hand over his heart. "But it has to be from here to make it good. I'm only just now discovering that for myself."

"Words, Gabriel. That's all they are...words, and very easy for you to say. But I've spent thirty-three years facing the realities all around me, and believe me, the one thing I know better than anything else is that we don't always get what we want. In some cases, we don't *ever* get what we want."

"And what is it you want?" he asked, fighting off the urge again to simply pull her into his arms. Even if he couldn't make it better for her, *or for himself*, he did want to hold her, to let her know that somebody cared. She was so wounded, and so fiercely defensive about keeping people away from her, yet the woman standing there at the door, ready to bolt, didn't fool him at all. Not for a minute. She wanted what he wanted to give her and, unless he was totally mistaken, she loved him. But she didn't know how to receive it and if, in the future, there was to be anything between them, it would have to be her opening herself up. Anything else that he might force on her would be like trying to cover an abdominal incision with a finger bandage. It would work in a small area but it wasn't enough to hold everything together. With her, he wanted everything held together, and he did have the right bandage. But she would have to be the one to apply it. Or ask him to apply it for her. And right now she still believed that tiny finger bandage was enough, and there was nothing he could do about that.

"I want my sister back." She brushed back the tears sliding down her cheeks. "That's what I want."

"Isn't there more?" Dear God, this hurt him. He hated inflicting the pain, but this was like the surgeries he performed. When something was wrong that needed correcting—an appendix removed, a tumor cut out—he would cut open his patient and perform the necessary procedure. Then came the healing, which did hurt, but eventually the pain went away and what was left was better than what had been there prior to the surgery. In her life, Arabella had never gotten to the part where the pain went away. She'd had all the surgeries, all the pain that went with them, and that's where it had all stopped for her. She'd never had *any* closure, and that had turned into more guilt than any one person should ever have to bear. Especially over things that weren't her fault. "What do you want for yourself, Arabella? And don't say work, because we know that's just something you hide behind."

"I don't know what you mean!"

Ah, the wall again. And just when he'd thought he was getting through. "I think you do," he said gently. "I believe you know exactly what I mean."

"OK. I want to stay here. Open a clinic, fulfill Rosie's promise. That's what I want, Gabriel. All I want."

Bella elevated stubborn to an art form and it was clear from the unappeasable look on her face now that he could argue and reason and persuade until he ran out of breath, and it wasn't going to do a damn bit of good. Bella was being… Bella. If he ever got beyond the point where they were locking horns day and night, that was something he was going to have to love. Simply love. Heart of gold buried beneath an awful lot of stubborn gristle.

And, damn, he liked that. Liked the challenge. Liked the reward he knew was buried there. "I think the whole area would be very lucky to have you, if that's what you really want to do. But that's not what I wanted to know, and since we're getting nowhere…" He brushed around her and opened the door. "I want to know what *you* want, Arabella. But you have to be the one who tells me, and because you want to tell me—not because I force it out of you."

Just a few steps into the hall he turned back and finally did what he'd wanted to do all along. He pulled her into his arms, and kissed her, not in a friendly little gesture as he'd done before but in the way a man needed to kiss a woman. Crushing her hard to his body, he lowered his head to her and sought her lips with a hunger that surprised him. Opening her mouth with his tongue, he sought the deep recesses, felt her respond with her own tongue, heard just the slightest whimper of a moan escape her as she wound her fingers around his neck and held him there. Pressed her hips to his in a way that caused him to go erect immediately and groan aloud, with no thought whatsoever about where they were and who might be watching them.

He reached out his left hand to touch her face, to feel her skin, craving that connection, that intimacy. And she allowed it for a moment, allowed him to run his thumb down her delicate jaw and down her throat to that hollow spot he longed to kiss…that, and so much more of her. All of her. Then, suddenly, she pulled back, her eyes raked over him, toes to head, very slowly, very deliberately, making love to him in a way he'd never imagined possible. So sensually. So completely in just one look.

Her breaths were uneven, her nipples hard and straining against the thin fabric of her cotton shirt as she took him in. And all he could do was stand there. Silent. Almost in a trance. Allowing her all the journey she wanted.

When she was finished, when she reached his face, and their eyes locked—hers so defiant, and hurt, and so full of love and open want—that's when he knew every answer, even to the unasked questions. It wasn't going to be easy, but if took the rest of his life, he would have this woman.

Still without a word she stretched out her right hand and ran it over his chest, and even through his shirt she caused him chills like no woman had ever done. Then, when she reached up and brushed her fingers across his cheek, she finally spoke. "You're what I want, Gabriel. But you're also what I can't have. Not in Chicago, not here. And *that's* because I do love you."

CHAPTER NINE

"Who is it?" Bella asked. She was sitting cross-legged on the wooden floor, tending to one of the children.

Father Carlos shrugged. "A child from one of the villages. He said he has to see Juan Gabriel right away. But I don't know where he is."

Neither did Bella. After they'd parted, she'd spent several hours tending patients around the village, while he did the same in the church, yet when she'd returned there he had gone, and no one seemed to know where. "He may have gone for a walk. I just don't know."

"Well, the boy is insistent. Maybe you could help him instead?"

"Where is he?"

"Outside. He won't come in. Says he wants to go back to his village after he sees Juan Gabriel."

"I'll be right out." After changing the bandage she'd been working on, one that was on the skinned knee of a little girl who needed the attention more than she needed the bandage, Bella stepped outside to see what she could do for the boy. He was about fifteen, she guessed. Very athletic. Very anxious to get back to his home, as Father Carlos had said.

"She told me I had to see Juan Gabriel." His English was surprisingly good.

"I'm a doctor, too," Bella said. "Could I help you?"

"But she said Juan Gabriel." He looked agitated, and not at all pleased with this change in his mission.

"Who said?"

"The lady. I don't know her name, but she said—"

"You have to see Juan Gabriel. I know. But I don't know when he's going to return. So you can wait, or I can take a look at you, if you trust me to help you."

He shook his head. "I'm not sick. I have a message. I have to give him a message."

"Could you give me the message, then I'll tell Juan Gabriel as soon as I see him?" She was getting impatient now. There was so much work to do, and if this boy wasn't willing to trust her…

"She took the baby with her," he said.

"What?"

"The baby. Ana Maria. The nurse took her."

This made no sense. "What nurse?"

"She comes to the villages sometime, looking for babies. She took Ana Maria. That's what the lady told me to tell Juan Gabriel."

"Gloria Elena?" Panic raised instantly. "Is that who sent you with the message?"

He nodded. "She wants Juan Gabriel to come right away."

Dear God, someone had taken Ana Maria! "Father!" she practically screamed at the priest, who was on his way to enter a house across the street.

"What it is?" he choked out, running over to her.

"Somebody took Ana Maria away from Gloria Elena. I don't have any details except that it was a woman, a nurse of some sort."

"*La Madre de Dios*," he whispered, his face blanching. "I don't let them come here. But they go to other villages, looking for babies to adopt out to families. It makes them much money to find a baby for a family. And some of the villagers…it's not a good way, but it happens sometimes."

"Someone approached Gabriel in Iquitos. She wanted Ana Maria, but he told her no."

"After the earthquake, there was much confusion. She came to take advantage of that confusion."

"But how?"

"The mountain has other roads to the villages. She could have traveled in easily, and with people coming *here* for medical help, or dealing with damages… Forgive me for saying this, but I believe she knew exactly how to take advantage of a terrible situation."

"By kidnaping babies when people are at their very worst?" This was insane! She had to do something *now* or Ana Maria could be lost forever. "Father, you've got to find Gabriel and tell him what's happened. I'm going to go to Gloria Elena."

"My car. It will take you half the way there. But I've heard that the road is blocked by trees." He fished car keys from his pocket and tossed them to her. *"Via con Dios,"* he said, then turned and ran into the church.

The first half of the trip to the tiny village called San Lourdes was slow, but the road was amazingly passable. Had the nurse found a passable road? Bella prayed that wasn't the case, prayed that she was stranded somewhere right now, unable to go any farther. Except, since she'd gotten up the mountain, then she knew the way back down. That caused a sinking feeling in the pit of Bella's stomach as she was finally forced to a stop by those trees Father Carlos had warned her about. She'd come a good two kilometers, but now she had to run the rest of the way, which turned out to be another kilometer. Unfortunately, while she was in what she considered to be fairly good shape, she didn't come close to keeping up with Pablo Espino, the boy who'd come for Gabriel. Pablo was quick, endowed with the speed of a distance runner, and it was quite obvious he was put out having to slow down to Bella's pace. But he did, making sure he kept well ahead of her. By the time they'd reached San Lourdes, she was so winded if felt like her chest was going to explode.

"Where's Arabella?" Gabriel called out the door to Father Carlos. "I need her to come take a look at George Gabriel. He's not…" He wasn't going to shout to the village priest that the newborn wasn't taking too well his mother's breast and what to do about it was totally out of his range of expertise. "I think she'll do better with this than I will."

He hadn't seen Bella for hours, but that was for the best. He'd needed breathing room, and time to think. But at first thinking hadn't helped because it had merely widened the chasm between them. The distance from Chicago to Lado De la Montaña was a big one, but the distance from his heart to hers was even bigger. And there was so much emptiness in it—emptiness like he'd never felt before.

He'd gone down to the stream to get away and spent an hour tossing pebbles into the water, trying to figure out just what he was doing. But there was nothing to figure out. He loved her. Head over heels, heart and soul. No convincing himself to do otherwise.

So the question became, whether he could live without her in Chicago, and the answer had come so quickly it had surprised him. No, he couldn't. Chicago was about things—his medical practice, his status, his nice condo on the lake, his car. Things. That's all! But Lado De la Montaña was about heart. And Arabella. And Ana Maria and his mother.

His *things* made life bigger. But the people in his life made his life better. So when he'd told Arabella that dedication was a good thing, but only when it was for the right reason, he'd been right. And so wrong. His dedication to his life in Chicago had only been for the things he had there, and they didn't matter, especially not when everything that did matter was right here in his little mountain village.

It had surprised him to realize that home truly was where the heart was, and his heart was here. But it was a good kind of surprise.

So, he'd stayed at the stream a while longer, thinking about the good memories he'd made here with his father, and planning for the good memories he'd make here with his daughter. And with Arabella. Although he realized that might take a lot of work—work he looked forward to since she, more than anything, was where his heart was.

Then he'd come back to do what he loved to do—taking care of patients. Not for the doctor's fees he'd earn, or the prestige that his medical practice would bring him. But for the pure love of medicine, which was what he saw in her every time he watched her work. She did love it. Her truest passion was there, and it was for herself, for doing the thing she loved best. He'd been wrong to accuse her of being dedicated for the wrong reason when, all along, he'd been the one dedicated to all the wrong things. Her dedication so far transcended the things that most people considered normal and reasonable that he was truly in awe. For her it was all about being needed as a doctor, and it didn't matter where that was. He wasn't sure she could see that in herself yet, but he did, and his new, true dedication was to help her find pure joy in her passion because she'd helped him rediscover the joy in his own. It was good to be home, and this truly was home. Finally.

"Can you go and find Arabella for me?" he called again to the priest, who was running frantically toward the Reyes house.

"She's gone to San Lourdes. Just a while ago..." He gasped for breath, bending over, hands on knees, trying to catch it

At the mention of San Lourdes, Gabriel's first thought was about his mother. Had something happened to her? Or to Ana Maria? "Why?" he choked out.

"It's the baby. She's gone."

"Ana Maria?" It wasn't sinking in yet. Wasn't making sense.

"A nurse came to the village after the earthquake and took her. That's all I know. We didn't know where you were, so Bella went."

"How long?"

"Half an hour ago. Maybe a little longer. They took my car and…" Father Carlos didn't bother finishing as Gabriel was already on his way down the road, looking for a vehicle to take him as far as the road would go. What he did do, however, was go to the church to pray.

San Lourdes was much smaller than Lado De la Montaña—not as many cars or houses. Not as many people on the street either. But Bella did notice a huddle of villagers surrounding one of the tiny houses, people shouting and animated, and she wondered if that's where she'd find Gloria Elena. As it turned out, she was correct. Gabriel's mother was inside, sitting in a straight-backed wooden chair, crying inconsolably, while a woman about her age fussed around her.

When Gloria Elena saw Bella she jumped up and fairly ran across the room to her. "Juan Gabriel is here?"

"Not yet," Bella said. "Father Carlos went to find him, and he'll be here soon." The women looked so stricken, her face so drained of all color, that Bella was instantly concerned. "What happened?" she coaxed, as she led her back to the chair.

"Ana Maria. She took Ana Maria." Her English was broken, her voice wobbly.

Bella knelt beside her and took her pulse. Fast, but not alarming. "The nurse?"

Gloria Elena nodded, and started to cry again.

"She told me she came for the baby," Doloros Cunya, Gloria Elena's cousin, said between her own tears. "She wore a uniform. I thought…I thought I was supposed to let her take Ana Maria. She said she was supposed to, that she'd talked to Juan Gabriel, so I let her." Sobs overtook her words, and Bella was getting frustrated because they were wasting time. But both women were inconsolable.

"I went to the church," Gloria Elena finally said. "Just for a few minutes. When I did…"

Now it was making sense to Bella. Gloria Elena had gone to the church and the woman they were calling the nurse had approached Doloros Cunya for the baby. A *nurse*, in a white uniform. Purposely deceptive. Probably waiting for her opportunity.

Doloros continued, "She was a nurse. I trusted her!" Her voice quivered off into a giant sob and she ran from the room.

"Gabriel," Gloria Elena choked.

"He'll be here," she assured the older woman. But Bella had the sinking feeling that it might be too late. "How would she get out of the village?"

Gloria Elena didn't answer, but one of the other women in the room stepped up. She was young, and very pregnant. Bella wondered if she might be the next victim of the woman in the white uniform. "Two roads," the woman said. "Only two."

The one *she* had taken to get here, which was blocked, and another one. "How long ago did she leave with the baby?"

There wasn't really consensus on that question, but Bella had the impression it had been somewhere between two and three hours. Maybe even four. Was that enough time to get to one of the larger cities? Or meet a contact who would take Ana Maria on to the next person?

"Is there a faster way to get out of here than by the road *the nurse* took?"

"Through the jungle," one of the women volunteered. "But that's dangerous, if you don't know your way."

Besides the obvious dangers, there was no way of knowing the woman's destination. A huge lump formed in Bella's throat. None of that mattered. She had to do something. But what?

Then it came to her. Dr. Navarro's office. Gabriel had mentioned that the nurse in Dr. Navarro's office had contacted an adoption agency, so she would know. She *had* to know. "I have to get to Iquitos," she said. "The fastest way possible." Maybe, just maybe, if the woman who'd taken Ana Maria was traveling by the road, it would be a slow trip for her owing to damage from the earthquake as well as the practical aspects of caring for a newborn.

"We can get to the road, but the fastest way is still through the jungle," Pablo volunteered. "I can take you, if you want. If you can run faster."

Run faster. Could she? "How long?"

He shrugged. "Slow, until we get to the road. Maybe three or four hours, if we hurry."

"Would it be faster going back to Lado De la Montaña and trying to get down the mountain from there?"

"No. I think if you follow me, it will be faster. I know some different ways down, if you're not scared going off the trail."

Off the trail and without her big stick. Well, there wasn't a sane choice to be found here. There wasn't *any* choice. "Let's go." Bella gave Gloria Elena's hand a squeeze, then spoke to one of the women with a better grasp of English. "Have someone go tell Father Carlos that the nurse who works in Dr. Navarro's office might know where they're taking Ana Maria. Tell him to have the authorities in Iquitos find her. Also tell Father Carlos that I'll need fast transportation when we get to the road, if he can arrange it." If anyone could do that for her, it would be the resourceful priest. Chasing *the nurse* down the mountain, hoping to cut her off somewhere, or even getting to Iquitos in time to find help… Those weren't good plans. In fact, they weren't plans at all. Just desperate reactions to a horrible situation. But sometimes you had to act first, then let the plans catch up. *You were right, Rosie.* "And if you see Gabriel, tell him…tell him I love him."

At the beginning of their trip through the jungle, Pablo stayed much closer to Bella than he had earlier, although they didn't converse.

Concentrating on what they were doing was their only focus as they pounded their way over the ground, sometimes on the trail, sometimes off. It wasn't easy for a jungle-dumb doctor from San Francisco who never even walked in the park, but at the end of the first hour Pablo led her into what seemed to be a fairly dense area of underbrush. Some he hacked away with a machete he carried…a machete that reminded her of Gabriel. And some they merely trampled underfoot.

Somewhere into their second hour, Pablo stopped, and pointed to an outcropping of rocks jutting up from the earth. "Sit," he said. "You rest for a while while I go ahead to clear the trail."

Sit, all alone in the jungle. Being guided by someone who wasn't much more than a boy, and trusting him with her life. Because if they got lost…well, she wasn't going to think about that. She just had to trust. And hope for one of those miracles she didn't believe in. That's all there was. So she sat there, watching a family of scarlet, red and green macaws bobbing in and out of the crags in the clay-colored rocks, nesting and tending to little ones, and totally unconcerned by her presence there. A large black beetle-like bug, nearly the size of her fist, wandered dangerously close to the toe of her shoe, and, like the macaws, didn't seem all that concerned by her presence. Didn't it have some instinct warning it that one tap of the toe of her shoe and she'd crush it? Didn't the macaws sense that if she wanted, she could reach out and pluck their babies from the nest?

Life was so precarious. For the bugs, or the birds…for her, and Gabriel. No matter what, life was always on the edge, so easy to tip one way or another. Sometimes, maybe even most of the time, the way it tipped was not under any particular control or, at least, not under the control of the person who wanted to control it. That black bug could have walked well away from her, and in its estimation avoided the possibility of being crushed. Or it could have hidden itself in the leaves, feeling protected there, only to have her step on it accidentally because she hadn't seen it. For that bug, to live was to run head on into risks everywhere.

And to survive was a miracle. Just thinking of Ana Maria in the arms of the woman who was stealing her… Dear God, she had to save that baby. No matter what, she had to bring Ana Maria back. Give her to Gabriel, and…

And be that baby's mother.

For the love of Gabriel, and for Ana Maria, she could go to Chicago. They were what mattered. All that mattered. And she could fulfill Rosie's dream another way. Use Rosie's money to open that clinic and find other doctors to run it.

It was all so simple when she let it seep in. Gabriel had said there was another side if she wanted to see it. "You were right," she whispered, as she watched the bug disappear under a log. Loving Gabriel and Ana Maria was everything.

It *was* a miracle, wasn't it? They really did happen. And now she needed another miracle, a big one that brought her baby back to her and Gabriel.

"Dr. Bella," Pablo cried from down the trail. "I found it. Hurry. Come quickly. I found it."

"Found what?" Bella yelled, jumping to her feet. She took off running down the trail Pablo had carved out for her, as vines and branches reached out from the trail's edge to slap her and cut her arms, wondering what she was chasing after other than her young guide.

"Over here," Pablo called. "Hurry."

He was off trail, in a particularly dense patch of undergrowth, and Bella thought it odd that he was beckoning her in that direction, but she trusted him to get her where she needed to go, so she veered into a dark, damp tangle of ferns and other vegetation she couldn't identify, swatting away the cloud of gnats and mosquitoes that wanted to swarm her face as she ran. Twice she tripped over thick vines growing across the ground, but didn't fall. Once she tripped and fell, then got back up and kept on pushing herself through toward Pablo.

But as she got closer, a cold, down-to-the-bone chill shot through her and she stopped. Couldn't move. Couldn't breathe. Then the jungle started swirling around her. Was it another earthquake, or was her head just growing light? She didn't know. Couldn't tell. But the cold suddenly melted away and she felt…overwhelmed. And protected. And loved.

"Rosie," she whispered.

Her sister was here. Everything she'd wanted to find. And had dreaded.

"Dr. Bella, look!"

She felt Rosie's arms wrap around her, felt her love. Felt everything she'd needed for so very long. Shutting her eyes, Bella allowed herself to feel all of it, to let it sink in. Rosie's love, her pain, her choices. "I wasn't ready to let you go, Rosie. I've fought against it all this time. But now…I have to."

"Please, Dr. Bella. Come look over here."

"I've missed you so badly," Bella whispered. "And I'm so sorry for the way we argued those last few weeks. But I understand now. I know what it's like to follow your heart wherever it takes you."

"Dr. Bella, I can see some of the plane from here."

"I didn't know how to go on without you. Didn't want to, Rosie. I've been so lost and confused, and it hurt so much I wanted to die, too." Bella wrapped her arms around herself, willing an image of Rosie to appear in her mind. But it wasn't Rosie's face she saw. It was Ana Maria's. "My baby," she whispered. She had to get to her baby.

She'd come to Peru to find her sister, but that didn't matter now. And Rosie wouldn't have had it any other way. Bella understood that now. Truly understood it. "I love you," she whispered, as she motioned Pablo over to her. "But it's time for me to move on." She'd told Natali Diego it was time to let go, and now it was her time. "Thank you, Rosie," she said, choking back the tears. "Thank you for loving me and for being my sister. I'll always love you…"

Yes, it was time. She felt at peace with the decision. More than that, she felt at peace with herself. Maybe for the first time in her life.

"You don't want to see the plane? Gloria Elena said you came here to find the plane."

He was clearly perplexed, but she was not. "We can't help them, Pablo. They're…" In the past. "They're gone now. And we need to find my baby." Leave the past in the past and move on toward the future.

"I'm sorry," Gabriel said, stepping up behind her and pulling her into his arms.

"I knew you would find us," she whispered, lingering in his embrace for but a moment, taking everything she needed from it to give her the strength to move on.

For the next hour, the three of them ran without speaking, conserving energy by saving breath, but Bella felt renewed as they ran the last leg of their short-cut through the jungle, Pablo leading the way, her in the middle, Gabriel just behind her. And as they emerged on the road leading to Iquitos, which was still a good way up the mountain and a long way from Iquitos, they had only half a kilometer to run before they found an old truck waiting for them. An old man from one of the villages below the mountain was waiting, insisting that he would drive, while Bella and Gabriel squeezed in next to him. Pablo declined to go, probably because he was anxious to get back to his village to tell everybody how he'd discovered the plane wreckage.

So, once they were all en route, with Luis at the wheel, bumping and jerking down the road, Bella slipped her hand into Gabriel's. It was an inadequate gesture, but given the circumstances it was all she could do. "We'll find her," she said, even though her voice was practically drowned out by the clanking of the motor. "I sent word to Father Carlos to have the authorities get Dr. Navarro's nurse. She'll know, Gabriel. Since she was part of this, she'll know."

Brave words that she truly didn't feel. But Gabriel nodded, even though he didn't take his fixed stare off the road while they dodged the ruts and swerved around the biggest rocks.

Several kilometers down the road they

overtook another vehicle having the same trouble they were. It was a small car, moving along at a really slow speed even under these bad conditions.

"Can you pass them?" Bella asked impatiently.

Luis shrugged, clearly not understanding what she meant.

"Pass them," Gabriel translated, to which Luis responded with a big, wide grin, then stamped on the gas pedal. Stamping only increased the speed by a fraction, but Luis swerved out to pass the small vehicle, and honked the horn as they pulled alongside it. Bella glanced over at the woman, who slowed down even more to let them pass. She was fighting her steering-wheel, both hands gripped tight on it, looking straight forward. She didn't even glance over as the truck pulled next to her, then went ahead. But Bella did. And that's when she saw it. The woman was wearing white.

The nurse!

"Stop," she shouted. "Right now, stop!" She was scrambling over Gabriel's lap and out the door before the truck had come to a standstill, and running back toward the car, which was slowing to a stop now, too.

The woman inside rolled down her window, but Bella didn't give her time to speak. She simply yanked open the back door and climbed in, then pulled Ana Maria from the car seat. "My baby," she cried, hugging the baby to her chest, then handing her out to Gabriel. "Our baby." A true miracle.

"I've talked to the police, and they've taken my nurse, Melaina Juarez, into custody. She says she knows nothing about this adoption agency, but I think she'll tell me." Dr. Raul Navarro was clearly suffering over this. "I'm so sorry about this, Gabriel. If I'd known…"

"It's not your fault," Gabriel replied. He wasn't going to vent his anger on the man. Raul had enough problems now, brought on by his office nurse. And, as it turned out, the woman Raul had also intended to marry. He was a good man and, as much as Gabriel wanted to kick the walls and scream, it wouldn't serve a purpose. They had Ana Maria back now, and Bella was checking over her in one of Raul's exam rooms.

"But it happened in my office, by my…"

Gabriel patted Raul on the shoulder. "I'm sorry, too."

"I'll let you know what happens," Raul said on his way out the door. "And, please, if there's anything I can do…anything…"

The poor man would be needing a lot of help himself. Gabriel felt sorry for him.

"Ana Maria's fine. Fit, happy and not even fussy." Bella carried the baby over to Gabriel. "The nurse did take care of her. I think that's why she drove so slowly, to protect her."

Gabriel took Ana Maria into his arms and held her like he'd never held her before. "She took good care of her because she was going to sell her." He pulled the receiving blanket back and stared into Ana Maria's face for a moment, then gave her a tender kiss on the forehead. "Those were the worst hours I've ever spent in my life. I almost lost her, and what you did…"

"*We* almost lost her," Bella corrected. She stepped into his arms, and the two of them embraced Ana Maria together, and embraced each other. "I now know this ends," she whispered. "I finally know."

"So do I."

"Since the authorities are going to get word to Father Carlos, who will get word to your mother, maybe we could go to the hotel for the night. Just the three of us." A family. *Her family.* "There are so many things I need to tell you, like I love you, I love you, I love you…"

"Are you going for one hundred?" he asked, laughing.

"One hundred or more. I love you, I love you, I love both of you…"

EPILOGUE

"IT'S a good place for her," Bella said, standing at the gate to the little village cemetery with Gabriel. "I think Rosie would like being next to Lynda." Her sister had a headstone now and Bella had gone to the grave several times these past few weeks, along with Gabriel, who was finally able to go to his own sister's grave. It had taken the strength of two for either of them to face these realities, but they had found that strength in each other.

Life was settling down in Lado De la Montaña. Homes were being rebuilt, lives being restored. In another week she would return to San Francisco to close her apartment and end her life there. Then she would return here to start a clinic. With Gabriel. Her husband.

Father Carlos had insisted on conducting their wedding vows shortly after they'd returned to the village with Ana Maria. The wisdom he'd imparted, after he'd informed the good people of Lado De la Montaña to prepare the church for a wedding, was, "Why wait? You love each other, that's not going to change. So why put it off, especially when the whole village is involved in it now? After so much sadness here, this is bringing them such happiness."

Father Carlos did have his persuasive, uncanny ways, because a week later, in a simple ceremony with new friends and new family, she and Gabriel had wed. "I think I understand how Rosie felt," Bella had said, as they'd crossed the road to watch several men from the village nail together the boards of what would be their new clinic in a few weeks. "When that woman took Ana Maria…everything changed. I would have done anything to get her back. It was what I had to do, but not because I was obligated. That's all my heart knew. Like Rosie's heart. She had to come here, and that's all she knew."

"You did everything for Ana Maria, even risked your life because you didn't know what Señora Hernandez would, or could do."

The authorities had taken her into custody peacefully, as the "nurse" had protested all the way that Gabriel had given away the baby.

Maybe it was a misunderstanding, but Bella didn't think so. It was in the hands of the local authorities now, and she wasn't dwelling on the unpleasantness anymore. Not with so many good things in her life now. "And me in the jungle without my stick. But I'm warning you right now, don't count on me playing queen of the jungle again for a very long time. I've still got bug bites the size of Ana Maria's little fist." She pointed to a very tiny faded red spot on her cheek where she'd been bitten. The bite itself had long since healed, but she liked to remind him because when she did, she reaped a fine reward. "Right here," she prompted.

He kissed her there, then found another imaginary bug bite to kiss, and another.

"I like the way you take care of your patients, Dr. Velascos," she purred.

"And I like the way my patients like to be taken care of, Dr. Velascos."

"You don't mind staying here?" She'd told him she'd go to Chicago, because she would have. Home was with Gabriel and Ana Maria, wherever they were. Her real home.

"I couldn't stay anywhere else. Once I realized what truly mattered, this was my home again, and it's the only place I want to be. Here, with you and Ana Maria." He patted her flat belly. "And maybe another Velascos baby in a year or two." He chuckled. "Besides, you're somewhat of a local legend now, and I like basking in your glory."

"What you like basking in are all the *alfajores, turrones,* and *lúcuma* ice cream Señora Alcantara sends over every day." She patted his belly back.

He responded to her pat by leaning over and kissing her on the neck. "Well, maybe that, too! But that's not what I really prefer to bask in. I have other favorites, if you'd like me to remind you."

"It *is* good, isn't it? I mean everything. Us, together. Our family. Friends. The clinic we're building." Named after her sister.

"It's very good, Arabella. What's also good is that it didn't take me forever to convince you to marry me. Once Father Carlos convinced you that it was a very practical plan…"

"Father Carlos?"

Grinning, Gabriel shrugged. "I suppose there were other factors. And it *was* practical."

"There was nothing at all practical about it, Gabriel. In fact, it was more like…"

"Catching a dream?"

"Or a miracle. Or both." She'd become a believer. Rosie had taught her how. So had Gabriel. "You know, when I was going to find Ana Maria, I think that's the first time I ever truly understood the kinds of amazing things people do for those they love. And it's not really a sacrifice if you love them. I always thought Rosie sacrificed so much for me, but it's what she wanted to do. Maybe even had to do. I didn't understand that until I knew that there wasn't anything I wouldn't do to get Ana Maria back. So maybe the biggest miracle of all was realizing that when you love someone, you don't think of it as a sacrifice or an inconvenience. Finding Ana Maria helped me find my sister and, more than that, helped me find things in myself I never knew were there."

"I knew they were there. Anybody who knew you saw them, Arabella. When you were calling yourself selfish, what everybody else saw was selfless."

"That's being too generous. I still have so many things to deal with. So many feelings. Things to reconcile." But they didn't seem so big, or overwhelming, any more. There was still guilt to resolve, and she knew that in her down moments she might tend to revert back to the old Bella. But she had so much support now, people she loved, people she trusted. And she had Gabriel. That he believed in her made her *almost* believe she could believe that much in herself. It would be a slow process, but she trusted Gabriel when he promised she'd get there. For the first time in her life, she wanted to.

Life was good in a way she'd never believed she could have for herself. In a few short weeks Arabella Burke, lonely lady, had become Arabella Burke Velascos, married lady, with a baby. *Be spontaneous, Bella. I know that goes against your nature, but be spontaneous with this change in plans. Step outside your normal self just this once. Have some fun. Who knows? Maybe something absolutely wonderful will happen when you least expect it.*

"It did, Rosie," she whispered. "It truly did."

MEDICAL™

Large Print

Titles for the next six months…

January

THE VALTIERI MARRIAGE DEAL	Caroline Anderson
THE REBEL AND THE BABY DOCTOR	Joanna Neil
THE COUNTRY DOCTOR'S DAUGHTER	Gill Sanderson
SURGEON BOSS, BACHELOR DAD	Lucy Clark
THE GREEK DOCTOR'S PROPOSAL	Molly Evans
SINGLE FATHER: WIFE AND MOTHER WANTED	Sharon Archer

February

EMERGENCY: WIFE LOST AND FOUND	Carol Marinelli
A SPECIAL KIND OF FAMILY	Marion Lennox
HOT-SHOT SURGEON, CINDERELLA BRIDE	Alison Roberts
A SUMMER WEDDING AT WILLOWMERE	Abigail Gordon
MIRACLE: TWIN BABIES	Fiona Lowe
THE PLAYBOY DOCTOR CLAIMS HIS BRIDE	Janice Lynn

March

SECRET SHEIKH, SECRET BABY	Carol Marinelli
PREGNANT MIDWIFE: FATHER NEEDED	Fiona McArthur
HIS BABY BOMBSHELL	Jessica Matthews
FOUND: A MOTHER FOR HIS SON	Dianne Drake
THE PLAYBOY DOCTOR'S SURPRISE PROPOSAL	Anne Fraser
HIRED: GP AND WIFE	Judy Campbell

MEDICAL™

Large Print

April

ITALIAN DOCTOR, DREAM PROPOSAL	Margaret McDonagh
WANTED: A FATHER FOR HER TWINS	Emily Forbes
BRIDE ON THE CHILDREN'S WARD	Lucy Clark
MARRIAGE REUNITED: BABY ON THE WAY	Sharon Archer
THE REBEL OF PENHALLY BAY	Caroline Anderson
MARRYING THE PLAYBOY DOCTOR	Laura Iding

May

COUNTRY MIDWIFE, CHRISTMAS BRIDE	Abigail Gordon
GREEK DOCTOR: ONE MAGICAL CHRISTMAS	Meredith Webber
HER BABY OUT OF THE BLUE	Alison Roberts
A DOCTOR, A NURSE: A CHRISTMAS BABY	Amy Andrews
SPANISH DOCTOR, PREGNANT MIDWIFE	Anne Fraser
EXPECTING A CHRISTMAS MIRACLE	Laura Iding

June

SNOWBOUND: MIRACLE MARRIAGE	Sarah Morgan
CHRISTMAS EVE: DOORSTEP DELIVERY	Sarah Morgan
HOT-SHOT DOC, CHRISTMAS BRIDE	Joanna Neil
CHRISTMAS AT RIVERCUT MANOR	Gill Sanderson
FALLING FOR THE PLAYBOY MILLIONAIRE	Kate Hardy
THE SURGEON'S NEW-YEAR WEDDING WISH	Laura Iding

MILLS & BOON®

millsandboon.co.uk Community

Join Us!

The Community is the perfect place to meet and chat to kindred spirits who love books and reading as much as you do, but it's also the place to:

- **Get the inside scoop from authors about their latest books**
- **Learn how to write a romance book with advice from our editors**
- **Help us to continue publishing the best in women's fiction**
- **Share your thoughts on the books we publish**
- **Befriend other users**

Forums: Interact with each other as well as authors, editors and a whole host of other users worldwide.

Blogs: Every registered community member has their own blog to tell the world what they're up to and what's on their mind.

Book Challenge: We're aiming to read 5,000 books and have joined forces with The Reading Agency in our inaugural Book Challenge.

Profile Page: Showcase yourself and keep a record of your recent community activity.

Social Networking: We've added buttons at the end of every post to share via digg, Facebook, Google, Yahoo, technorati and de.licio.us.

www.millsandboon.co.uk